BLOOD BROTHERS

Sullivan was playing possum as the Gonzales brothers, Jesus, Jose and Hector, dragged him along the ground. Peering through hooded eyes, Sullivan saw his .44 swing past in Hector's left hand.

"Yo, thas a nice shootin' iron, man. You gonna keep that?" Jose asked.

"Sure man, he owes me that," Hector replied. Then the dragging stopped. "I think he's still alive, Tony."

Tony? thought Sullivan. Tony the Chill?

Hector screamed as Sullivan jumped him, grabbing the .44 and pulling Hector's body on top of him as a shield. Tony the Chill was gone, but Jesus caught it in the throat and Jose went down with a round in each lung. Sullivan then placed the weapon at Hector's skull and sent his brains into the air in a shower of red and gray.

Now for Tony the Chill, mused the Specialist, as he rolled the corpse off himself. . . .

ONE-MAN ARMY

In this book you will find a thrilling, danger-packed chapter from *Vengeance Mountain*, the ninth novel in the exciting adventures of **THE SPECIALIST**.

Ø

Exciting Reading from SIGNET

THE #8
SPECIALIST

ONE-MAN ARMY

John Cutter

A SIGNET BOOK

NEW AMERICAN LIBRARY

PUBLISHER'S NOTE

This novel is a work of fiction. Names, characters, places, and incidents either are the product of the author's imagination or are used fictitiously, and any resemblance to actual persons, living or dead, events, or locales is entirely coincidental.

NAL BOOKS ARE AVAILABLE AT QUANTITY DISCOUNTS
WHEN USED TO PROMOTE PRODUCTS OR SERVICES.
FOR INFORMATION PLEASE WRITE TO PREMIUM MARKETING DIVISION,
NEW AMERICAN LIBRARY, 1633 BROADWAY,
NEW YORK, NEW YORK 10019.

Copyright © 1985 by John Cutter

The first chapter of this book
previously appeared in *The Vendetta*,
the seventh volume in this series

Ⓢ

SIGNET TRADEMARK REG. U.S. PAT. OFF. AND FOREIGN COUNTRIES
REGISTERED TRADEMARK—MARCA REGISTRADA
HECHO EN CHICAGO, U.S.A.

SIGNET, SIGNET CLASSIC, MENTOR, PLUME, MERIDIAN AND NAL BOOKS
are published by New American Library,
1633 Broadway, New York, New York 10019

First Printing, April, 1985

1 2 3 4 5 6 7 8 9

PRINTED IN THE UNITED STATES OF AMERICA

1
A Hot Date with Death

He knew something was wrong when she didn't answer the door buzzer.

Jack Sullivan stood in the March drizzle on the stoop of the old brownstone building, ringing the bell, waiting for Bonnie Roland to reply on the intercom. There was no reply. He stepped back and looked up at her fifth-floor office. The old brownstone had been converted into apartment units. All of the windows, except one, were dark now. If he remembered right, the illuminated window was hers.

She had said, "I'll be at my office at nine P.M. You can count on it."

"It's a date," he had answered.

She'd laughed and said, "You think I'm going to date *you* again, Jack Sullivan? No way! This is business."

But they'd both known she hadn't meant it. They hadn't seen each other in more than a year. But they knew that what they'd had between them would still be there.

And they both knew she wanted to see him for other reasons, too. She was in trouble.

A year before, after she'd walked out on him, he'd sent a card to the office of her detective agency, Open Window Investigations. He'd given her a post-office-box number where she could reach him. Just in case she ever wanted to reach him again.

He checked the box once a month and this month it had contained a letter that said only, "I'm in deep this time and it's about to hit the fan. Need your help. Call my office if you want to help, and we'll meet. Bonnie Roland." She had closed the letter with her phone number.

But she wasn't answering her bell. Okay, maybe it was broken. Only . . .

Sullivan shook his head. It felt wrong. Something was out of kilter. She was an efficient woman. She'd have let him know if the bell was broken. And the light was on. And she'd said she needed his help.

And people only asked for Jack Sullivan's help when they were in bad trouble. Bad, mean, ugly trouble. The kind that kills.

Because Jack Sullivan was a specialist. He was *the* Specialist.

Sullivan was a big man. A barrel-chested, muscular man. But he could move with a dancer's agility when he had to. Now he turned and climbed atop the black iron fence around the brownstone, balanced on the two-inch metal bar between the spikes for a moment, then bent his legs and leapt up to catch the bottom rung of the fire-escape ladder. He hung there for a moment, then did a chin-up and looped an arm over the rung, grabbed the next one, pulled himself up.

A minute later he was loping up the metal stairs. In his hand was a .44 Automag, a big black pistol sometimes called "The Flesh Shredder." The series-C Automag fired a 240-grain bullet. Muzzle velocity: 1,640 fps. Muzzle energy: 1,455 pounds. The big slug from the four-pound Automag could tear through two inches of steel. It was almost a rifle. And he'd had it modified to carry ten rounds.

He slowed at the fourth floor, began to move more cautiously, anticipating trouble.

He reached the fifth floor. The iron of the fire-escape

rail was cold and wet under his left hand, the steel of the Automag cool and hungry in his right. Somewhere in the background, Manhattan droned insanely to itself as it does every Friday night; about movies and Broadway shows and cocktails and dope and parties and girls and more girls. Sirens wailed about accidents and heart attacks and shootings . . . planes rumbled about going places . . . ghetto blasters thumped about boogying. . . .

The rain sizzled down, heavier by the second. It distorted his view through the office window. But he saw enough.

He saw four men in ski masks. He saw a woman, almost certainly Bonnie. Tall, slender, leggy, strawberry-blond, green-eyed Bonnie. She was sitting in a chair. Tied to it. The four men stood around her, two in front, two behind. Two of them had guns showing. The other two were carrying lead pipes.

The guys with the pipes stood in front of her, slapping the pipes meaningfully into their palms. One of them bent near her, maybe to ask her a question. She shook her head. He straightened, and whacked her across the side of the face with the pipe. Not hard enough to break any bones. But hard enough to suggest that he'd start breaking bones soon enough.

Sullivan tensed, seeing them hit her. Fury boiled up in him. But he held himself in check, thinking hard.

What made him hold back was the guy behind her, on her right. He had his .38 pressed against the back of her head.

Sullivan was afraid to burst in—afraid the guy would pull the trigger if he were startled.

One of the guys in the red ski masks, standing in front of her, bent to ask her another question.

She shook her head.

He hit her again. Harder this time.

Sullivan couldn't bear any more of this. He was going to have to go for a clean kill, shooting the thug so that he would not jerk spasmodically in death.

He raised the Automag, gripped it with both hands,

and sighted in on the ski-masked man with the gun to Bonnie's head. He centered the sights on the base of the guy's skull, behind his left ear. Sever the medulla oblongata and he'd drop without so much as squeezing his trigger.

There was blood running down the side of Bonnie's face.

The big guy in front of her was raising the lead pipe again, higher this time, intending to break something with this one. . . .

Sullivan frowned, trying to sight in. The rain-warped image jumped around. If he wasn't accurate, the shot could cost Bonnie her life.

Sullivan squeezed the trigger.

The big Automag boomed and jerked viciously in Sullivan's hands. The glass shattered inward.

In the office, the gunman's head exploded—erupting behind the left ear. The close-range shot ripped away half his head and knocked him flying, off his feet and dead before he hit the floor, the gun tumbling from his fingers unfired.

The second gunman staggered back, startled, raising his gun and swinging it to home in on the stranger in the window.

Sullivan leapt through the remains of the window, broken glass flying around him in a jagged cloud, firing as he came. The second gunman went down, a .44 round from the Specialist's Automag blowing his teeth out through the back of his head; the pipe-wielder closest to Sullivan swung at the intruder. Sullivan, coming down on both feet in a crouch, tracked the gun across his body and fired point-blank, punching a hole through his sternum big enough to accommodate a man's thumb. The bullet emerged from his back, blowing out a ragged hole big as a grapefruit, pasting a couple of pounds of his bloody insides on the wall, the bullet following through to punch six inches into the plaster and wood before stopping.

The man was thrown back against the wall; he slid

down it, smearing blood on the white paint, his eyes behind the ski mask glazing.

The fourth thug was halfway through the door.

Sullivan whipped the gun around and fired—the slug ripped through the door and dug a deep red furrow across the man's chest—but the wound was superficial. The masked hardman grunted and kept going, sprinting down the hall.

Sullivan turned to Bonnie. "You okay?"

"Yeah, I'm okay—"

"You know who they are?" he asked as he pulled a switchblade from the pocket of his brown leather flight jacket and cut her loose.

"I think they work for a guy named Legion I've been investigating—"

"I'll see if I can confirm that."

He turned and stepped through the door, ran the way the thug had gone—to the right, for the stairs.

He rushed through the door leading to the stairs, and heard a door bang above. He'd gone to the roof!

Sullivan ran up the stairs and so he didn't hear Bonnie shouting after him. "Jack, wait a minute! They came from the roof and I think there's more of them up there!"

Sullivan emerged from the roof door, stepped out onto the tarpaper roof, a switchblade in his left hand and the .44 in the other.

A city roof at night is a strange combination of darkness and dazzle. Shadows lie thick across the roof's naked geometry—but city lights blink beyond. This building was overshadowed by three high-rises—one across the street and two to either side. Toward the rear was a construction site, a half-finished building rising like a skeleton four stories above the brownstone, steel girders glistening with rainwater.

There was a moment of quiet. Only the distant drone of the city, the swish of a breeze moving bits of paper trash across the roof . . .

And then the night exploded with gunfire.

Three men crouched behind a brick chimney forty feet ahead firing at him with handguns. Muzzle flashes lit the roof like flashbulbs, bullets cracked into the doorway—but the Specialist was already out of the line of fire. At the first shot, which ripped a hole through his coat at the left armpit and grazed his ribs, he'd thrown himself right, come down rolling, spun onto his feet, and leapt behind a metal vent shaped like the head of a cane. He was up and shooting before they'd tracked his position. He'd outflanked them.

He had a shooting angle at the one on the right, seeing him as an inky beast beside the shadow-shrouded hulk of the chimney. Sullivan squeezed off three rounds; the first one smacked into the chimney, knocking an entire brick loose. For the second round, his hands acting with years of refined reflexes, tracked left and down just a fraction of a centimeter. The next shot took the man cleanly through the side of his head. The third shot smashed through his partner's side.

The man screamed and fell writhing. The third man fired wildly at Sullivan. The slugs rang off the metal of the vent, sending up sparks.

Sullivan ducked down. When he looked up again the man was across the roof, firing over his shoulder.

Sullivan ran after him, slugs from the gunman's .38 whining through the air around him.

The man in the ski mask climbed onto the roof rim—and leapt.

Sullivan swore, amazed. It looked as if the guy had leapt off the roof into space.

But when Sullivan reached the edge of the roof, he saw that the construction site's nearest girder section was only seven feet off. The guy had leapt onto the unfinished building. There was a scaffolding over there, wide enough to jump onto. Sullivan looked down, peering down eight stories to the dirt alley between the site and the brownstone. He couldn't see a body over there. The guy had made it.

Sullivan shrugged. If some punk hit man could do it, he could do it too.

He stuck the .44 in his belt, clamped the knife in his teeth, backed up twenty feet, took a long run, and . . .

Leapt into space.

For a giddy moment he thought: Stupid. Should have let him go. Not going to make it.

And then the scaffolding rushed at him. He caught its upper railings and held on, felt himself slammed against its wooden slats by his own weight and momentum. He gasped, the air knocked out of him. He hung on, stunned, searching for breath. He made his lungs work, took a deep breath through his nose, the knife still clamped in his teeth.

He pulled himself up onto the scaffolding—and ducked, as a bullet scored sparks from a girder near his head.

He had seen the muzzle flash from the corner of his eyes. It was above and to the right. The guy had gone to high ground.

Sullivan moved to the left, putting the girder between himself and the gunman, and climbed off the scaffolding into a wooden walkway set up temporarily for the construction workers.

He took the knife from his teeth and looked up through the checkerboard of light and shadow, trying to spot the gunman.

There! Two unfinished floors above, running along another walkway toward a crane at the opposite corner. Maybe looking for a workman's elevator.

Sullivan ran along the lower walkway. To his right was a girder, and then empty air. To his left—just empty air. And a long fall. He reached the end of the walkway, found a ladder, and climbed it to the next level, and another ladder to the top.

He drew his gun, moved along the walkway toward the crane—and had to throw himself flat on the plywood as the crane swung toward him, whipping a two-hundred-pound steel hook on a three-inch-thick metal cable through the air at him. It slashed by just over his head.

The son of a bitch had the crane working. The enormous metal-grid arm swung ponderously back at him. One nudge from that sixty-foot steel arm and he'd be swatted out into space.

He ran on down the walkway, trying to get past the hook—but the man in the crane cab tilted the arm up so the huge, concrete-crusty hook swung after him, a two-hundred-pound pendulum that would splash him into nothing.

He had one chance.

He threw himself flat and rolled to the right. The hook sang past, barely missing him. For a moment, as it reached the end of its arc, it paused—and Sullivan leapt up and onto it.

He hung on, swinging sickeningly out over space, and then climbed up the cable hand over hand, hoping he could reach the crane's arm before the killer found the controls that would slacken the hook's cable.

He felt the cable begin to move—just as he reached the crane's arm. He pulled himself up onto the steel beams of the crane's outer arm section, and moved down it on all fours toward the cab. The glass-and-metal booth was just sixty feet away now. Fifty. Forty-five.

The murderous crane operator swung the crane hard right, stopped it, swung it abruptly left, trying to dislodge the Specialist.

Sullivan hung on bitterly, but the beams were slick with rainwater and the crane jerked him angrily, like a bird trying to shake an insect from its beak. He gripped the beams harder, till he felt the metal biting into his hand, and inched on, farther, farther, closer to the cab. . . .

The killer was climbing out of the cab now, trying to get a shooting angle.

Sullivan stood, and ran down the length of the arm, risking a fall, knowing he was a sitting duck out here.

The gunman fired at him. Bullets whined off the steel at his feet and zipped through the air around him.

And then he'd reached the cab. The gunman was on the other side, climbing into a wire-mesh workman's elevator. The elevator began to move. Sullivan cursed, and, leaning around the side of the crane cab, emptied his gun into the engine housing of the elevator behind the crane. The elevator spat sparks and smoke, and stopped.

Sullivan climbed through the cab and down the ladder beside the elevator.

Sullivan's gun was empty—but the gunman didn't know that. There was a girder between his perch on the ladder and the elevator. Sullivan reached around the girder and stuck his gun through the mesh in the small elevator.

"That's all," he said. "Come out or I empty it into you."

"All right—I'm gonna open the door!" the man shouted.

"Wait a minute, I think I like you better in there. You want to get out alive, tell me this: who the hell are you working for and why the hell are you leaning on my woman?"

"She's been on the tail of some landlord, guy named Legion. One of his men hired us to get some kind of file she's got on him."

"Okay, come on out." He withdrew the gun. "Throw your gun out. I've got the door covered."

There was a two-foot metal grate extending out from the bottom of the elevator. The gunman opened the door, stepped onto the metal grate, swung toward Sullivan with his gun upraised.

Sullivan had been ready for it. He'd stuck the .44 in his belt, gripped the ladder with his right hand. The switchblade was in his left hand, and he hooked it into the killer's chest before he could squeeze the trigger. He drove it expertly and with great experience sideways between the two ribs jut under the pectoral muscle on the left.

The gunman fired by reflex but he'd had no chance to aim. The bullet ricocheted from the metal ladder Sullivan clung to and the thug pitched forward, taking Sullivan's knife with him. He plunged eight stories to the cold ground.

Sullivan let out a long breath. Time to move. Cops would arrive soon.

He climbed down the ladder, his arms aching with the effort long before he reached the bottom. He saw the searching light of a watchman coming across the site. He dodged through the site to the back of Bonnie's building, trotted down the alley, and went around to the front. No cops here yet.

He pressed the bell.

This time she answered.

2

Lords of the Land or Scum of the Earth?

After the bandaging, the X rays and the EEGs, the doctors decided Bonnie was bruised but not seriously hurt, and Sullivan escorted her from the emergency room.

"How do you feel?" he asked as he drove her across town in his rented car. It was almost midnight. Emergency medical treatment doesn't come quickly in a New York City hospital.

"Weird. Probably because of the painkillers they gave me," Bonnie answered.

"You feel like filling me in on what happened? I got the name of the guy who hired those punks. Legion. And the fact that he was a landlord. That's about all I found out. I haven't been much use."

She smiled wearily at him. "You came when I needed you. You saved my life. I'd call that being useful. As for what happened—I guess it's like the story of the man who reached into a hole to catch a gopher and got his hand bitten off by a wolverine. I was hired by a guy named Terry Moreland. He's renting an apartment in a building on the Upper East Side. The landlord's trying to force the tenants out, evict them with a lot of pretenses so he can tear the place down and put up a high-price high-rise. Terry and a tenants' association managed to stop the landlord—"

"Legion."

"Right. Managed to stop Legion from legally evicting them. They hired a passel of lawyers. And there are a lot of laws controlling landlords in New York. So Legion tried other methods. He rented out the two vacant apartments to a bunch of junkies. They're constantly ripping people off. Then Legion hired other guys to vandalize the place, trying to make it unlivable. Tear off the front doors. Piss and shit in the hallways. Spray-paint the walls, knock out the hall lights, flood the place, bust up the stairs. The tenants' association called the cops, one of the vandals was arrested, and the tenants formed a security patrol. That slowed it down. Then Legion brought in some real hard cases. Started threatening the tenants, beating up on them. . . . So Moreland hired me, your friendly neighborhood Lady Private Eye, to come up with some legally provable connection between the thugs and Legion. My job is to get evidence he hired the guys to rough up the tenants, so we can put Legion in jail and the city'll take over the building."

"You must have gotten close," Sullivan said, taking a sudden right turn.

She looked at a street sign, then at Sullivan. "Where you going? I thought you were taking me home."

"I was. I changed my mind." He grinned at her. "You never saw those movies where the sheikh slings the beautiful woman of the north across his charger and gallops away to his secret oasis?"

"You call this a charger? I call it a Ford Bronco."

"A horse is a horse. . . . Anyway, I don't want you going back to your place. They know where you work, they probably found out where you live."

She nodded. "Your place?"

"You guessed it."

"The penthouse?"

"I'm afraid that was, ah, appropriated by police investigators. No, I'm staying at the Marriott."

"What? Aren't you supposed to be skulking down back alleys and wearing disguises and hiding in sleazy rat-holes on skid row?"

"Just because a few cops were after me?"

"The cops *after* you? Hell, Sullivan, they practically had the National Guard out doing a house-to-house search on the whole island!"

"That was many moons ago, my lady. The Justice Department has new plans for me, it seems. They want me to work in a special fed commando outfit. Some antiterrorist scam. So they took the heat off me, in exchange for . . . Well, I promised to consider it."

"I can't see you as a civil-service employee."

"No. It'd be 'half free-lance.' That's the phrase Sanson used. Briefing starts on February 10. So I've got a while. You hungry?"

She shook her head, then winced.

"Hurts when you shake your head? Don't nod to tell me yes. You know, you're pretty damn tough for—"

"Don't you dare say 'for a woman'!"

"Okay. But you are tough for a person of either gender. Most people'd be home whimpering after a beating like that."

"I'm too pissed off to whimper. I could use a drink, though."

"How about at the Marriott?"

She looked sideways at him. "In your hotel? I'm still thinking about that. You forgotten how we parted last time? You lying to me—"

"To get you out of harm's way. To save your life. Because I cared about you."

"Yeah. Maybe. But I called you because I need help—not because I need sex."

"Sex is a kind of help. And I can be *real* helpful."

She almost smiled. But then she said, "I know what you think. But I'm not easy."

He shrugged. "I think I'll rent you a separate room."

She looked at him. "You're smirking."

"Smirking? Me? No way."

"Smirking. And I know why. You think that just because we had incredibly good sex before, as soon as you and I are alone somewhere, maybe after a few drinks, I'm going to fall into your arms with a sigh and say, 'Ravish me!' "

"Hey give me a break—"

"I know what you think. Forget it. To use your phrase, no way."

Sullivan carefully held back a smirk.

The bar was warm and lit with indirect lighting. They sat in a red imitation-leather booth. To the right was a circular bar. Glasses glittered on racks, hung upside-down by their stems over the brass bartop. There was a soft murmur of conversation at the bar. An expensive "escort" with luxurious blond hair allowed her white-haired male companion to paw her knee as she sipped Dom Perignon from a champagne glass. Sullivan got tired of looking at the expensive whore and her well-paying, well-oiled customer and looked at Bonnie Roland.

"Even bruised," he murmured, raising his Scotch and soda in a toast.

She touched the bruises on her face lightly with the tips of her fingers. She sipped her Bloody Mary. "Maybe the bruises turn you on," she said.

He smiled. The smile didn't say yes or no.

"What've you got on Legion?" Sullivan said.

"Not a hell of a lot. But maybe I was asking in the right places. I wondered about his connection with the junkies. I mean, there was a whole troop of them. Where'd he find them? Did he just walk around the Lower East Side or Harlem and ask junkies if they needed a place to live? Not likely. He has some connection with them. The cops busted one of them for vandalism. I went to talk to him in jail. He was suffering. Bad junk withdrawal. Usually they can get on a methadone treatment program out at Riker's Island. But you got to grease the right wheels, and he didn't have any grease, and he'd pissed off one of the moguls in the jail by refusing to come across in the shower. So he didn't get his methadone and he suffered. I got a friend in the county drug treatment program. I told this junkie—his name was Costes—I could get him some government-provided heroin substitute, get him on a program, if he gave me some information on Legion. He refused to talk on my first visit. But when I came back three days later he was hurting bad, and he talked. I got a name and he got his methadone."

"What name?"

"Man named Crackwell. Said to collect money from heroin dealers. Said to be a middleman for Legion. I got another friend in NYPD records—"

"You got a lot of friends."

She smiled. "Cultivating useful friendships is a key skill for the private eye."

"These male or female friends?"

"None of your business. Anyway, my friend in NYPD got me photocopies of Legion and Crackwell. Crackwell has a file. Legion has a file—with nothing in it but his photos and reports from detectives who've heard rumors. My friend told me something else: the police are not at all surprised when they hear about Legion's antitenant goon squad. But they aren't moving on him in that department because they are trying to get the goods on him for heroin dealing. They have a projected plan for how they're going to nail him. They figure it'll take six months to a year. Or more. They want to get not only him but his whole network. The tenant arrest would net only him, and only temporarily. And it could spook him to cover himself, which would blow the investigation. There's another file on him, a bigger one, at the DEA offices. I can't get that."

"Maybe I can get it through Sanson."

"That'd help."

"I don't suppose there's any hope of you taking a walk on this thing. I mean, after tonight—"

"Forget it." Her voice was frosty.

"Okay. What'd you do to bring those bozos down on you?"

"Surveillance of Crackwell. Asking a lot of questions. I happened to ask one of his people on the streets. The scumbag reported back to Crackwell that I was trying to get the goods on the connection between Legion and Crackwell."

"Mmm." Sullivan signaled for another round. Bonnie hadn't yet finished her drink but he ordered another for her.

"What do you want me to do?" he asked when the waitress had come and gone.

"Not what you usually do. I don't want Legion killed unless it's in self-defense."

"Why? It'd be the simplest, most efficient way of dealing with the asshole."

"Because Moreland and the tenants' association could be implicated. And I do what I'm hired to do. They hired me to get the facts on him. That's all. And they want him alive, in court. They want to make an issue of it. Publicize landlord abuse of tenants."

"You can't always get what you want, to quote the Rolling Stones. But okay. So—I'm a bodyguard?"

"That's about the size of it. I need someone to stay at the building. Work with the tenants' association. Protect them. Keep the goons at bay. But, Jack—don't litter the streets with their bodies."

"I haven't said I'd take this on at all yet."

"We need to talk about money?"

He shook his head. "If it's for you, it's for free. Anyway, I've got money to last me a few years of high living, after the Reichstone gig. No—it's just that I don't like having my hands tied."

"Take it as a challenge. To beat them without killing them."

Sullivan shrugged. "Okay. You got yourself a bodyguard."

But Sullivan knew . . .

He knew that, sooner or later, he'd have to kill this man Legion. Because Legion had sent his goons around to lay into Bonnie Roland with lead pipes. Because they'd tied her up and humiliated her. And because they would've killed her.

Sullivan could feel it. The presence of real evil, just offstage, waiting in the wings. There were men involved in this who needed killing. And Sullivan knew that, eventually, these men would force his hand. It was as if Death were sitting beside Sullivan in the booth, whispering these things to him. It didn't bother Sullivan, sitting beside Death. They were old friends.

"When I looked through the window of your office," Sullivan said, "your charming visitors were asking you something. What was it they wanted to know?"

"Exactly who hired me. They knew it was one of the tenants, but they didn't know which one."

"Moreland."

"Yeah. I don't think you're going to like Moreland. He's liberal, maybe even leftist. Arty. Possibly gay."

"Long as he doesn't try to make me eat quiche. So what's next? I don't help you in the investigation?"

"Not for now. I want you to stay at their building. Watch over them, get them organized."

"And stay out of harm's way? Is this some kind of getting back at me?"

She grinned. "Maybe." She reached for her Bloody Mary.

An hour later they went to their respective rooms, across the hall from each other. It was a tastefully cream-colored hallway. They could smell the newness of the synthetic rug and the plaster. A television murmured from one of the rooms. Otherwise, nothing but dead quiet.

"I've got a bottle of champagne chilling in my room," he said.

"How'd you arrange that? You had it figured that—"

"No, no! The champagne is just, uh, for a good-night toast. It's good to see you again. We'll toast to old times and we'll go to our separate rooms. Or are you afraid to go in with me? Afraid you'll weaken?"

"Weaken? No fucking way. Point me to the champagne."

The champagne was waiting in its dewy bucket on a small chrome table beside the bed.

"There's a bar in this room," she pointed out. "Why's the champagne bucket next to the bed?"

"Must be room service jumping to conclusions," he said as he popped the cork and poured.

"Just don't *you* jump to any conclusions," she said.

"I'm a model of self-control."

"Tomorrow," she said, "you can move into Legion's building. One of the tenants is getting scared, he's leaving with a month left on his lease. He'll sublet to you."

"Okay. I'm paid up here for a week. You can stay in my place while I'm there. You need me, just whistle. You know how to whistle?"

"Just put your lips together and blow. What movie is that from?"

"I forget. Have some more champagne."

"Just one more glass. . . . Thanks. Mmm . . . Jack, thanks for coming. Thanks for helping."

He looked at her. Their eyes locked. She shivered. As if moving in a trance, she put the glass down, and stepped nearer to him. They were standing beside the bed. Two feet apart.

"You know what I said, Jack? About how I wasn't going to go along with this stuff about sighing and falling into your arms and begging you to ravish me?"

"What about it?"

"I was wrong."

She took the glass from his hand and put it on the table. "Hey," he said, "you were hurt tonight. You're in no shape to—"

He didn't say anything after that, because she had climbed up onto him as if he were a tree, wrapped her legs around him, and was pressing her tongue between his lips.

She writhed against him. He held her up in his arms now, pressing her to him. He turned and carried her to the bed. She tried to pull him down on top of her. He detached her arms from his neck and then slowly, carefully, meticulously undressed her. She lay on the bed all pink and ivory, except for raspberry-colored nipples which stood up, begging for attention. Her eyes glittered. One leg was cocked, and dampness glistened at the pink cleft between the two strips of blond hair at her pudenda.

"How dare you stand there fully dressed staring at my naked body," she said, her voice husky with pleasure, her eyes closed, as he looked her frankly up and down.

"What do you think?" she asked.

"I think I want you. Now. In fact, I know I do."

In a few moments he was undressed. He tossed her blouse over the bedside lamp so the room dimmed to a pleasant filmy glow. He stood beside the bed and reached out, letting his hands wander over her. Her flat belly, muscular under the silken skin. One hand reaching to wet labia, the other tracing the curve of her hip, the fine etching of her rib cage, skating over that smooth pearly skin up to her breasts, then cupping them to feel their warmth and the energy of her excitement pulsing in them. Ambidextrously he toyed with a breast and her clitoris at the same time, bending to kiss her on the belly, up between her breasts, up the long exquisite neck, brushing the satiny hairs, so fine they were hardly there, behind her ear, working his way to her lips, taking each lip in turn between his own and gently milking sensation from it. She groaned and pulled him atop her.

He knelt between her legs, his fingers, expert with every kind of trigger, squeezing her clitoris very gently. His big cock ramrod hard against her thigh. She moaned and directed his pink steel into her, drawing him nearer and rising to meet his thrusts with her pumping hips.

He bent to take her nipples in his mouth, first one and then the other.

He made love to her slowly and lingeringly and, keeping in mind what she'd been through that night, very gently.

Later, they finished off the champagne and fell asleep.

Sullivan dreamed he was walking along a jungle trail with Death. Death said, "You'll go from one kind of jungle to the other before you get him, Sullivan. Or before he gets you."

When Sullivan woke at dawn he thought about the dream. He knew there was some truth in dreams. He didn't want to know what the truth was in this one. He put it out of his mind, and got up to inventory his weaponry. It was a new day, and he had a job to do.

3
Guardian Angel, Guardian Demon

It was a Victorian brownstone, beginning to crumble around the edges. There were a couple of noseless cherubs under the cornices and floral bric-a-brac around the windows. It had been a handsome building once. Now it was faded to grimy gray-brown. One of the windows was boarded over. An old iron drainpipe hung askew from the roof. The fire escape was sagging. The front door was missing.

It was the right kind of day to visit that kind of building: the weather was foul as Sullivan and Bonnie got out of the Bronco and walked across the sidewalk. It was broken-umbrella weather. The wind spitefully changed directions when the mood struck it. It flung handfuls of rain in their faces as they climbed the six chipped stone steps to the front door.

Inside the hallway, Bonnie stood dripping on the bare floor. "There was linoleum on the floor," she explained, "but they tore it up." Bonnie wore a yellow raincoat tied at the waist, and a black knit pantsuit. Sullivan wore jeans, waterproof boots, and a brown leather trench coat. "All the graffiti started after Legion moved his creeps in." The walls crawled with obscenities in felt-tip and spray paint. There were a few warnings mixed in with the obscenities. "GET OUT OR GET KILLED," read

25

one scrawl. Another in bright red paint stated "WE GONNA BURN YOU OUT."

"And look here . . ." she said, leading him to a dark place under the stairs. There was a charred spot on the floor. "I think they set it when they knew Moreland was coming down. They knew he'd put it out. I'll bet Legion is paranoid of arson investigations, so he doesn't want to burn the whole building down unless he has to. Still, the fire under the stairs scared the tenants all right. That's why the place you're moving into is available."

A powerful thumping noise started up from the apartment on the right. A ghetto blaster throbbing out a disco beat so loud Sullivan could feel it in the bones of his skull. "That them in there?" he asked.

She nodded. "Let's go up and meet Terry."

He started for the elevator, but she shook her head. "They broke that too."

They climbed four flights to Terry Moreland's apartment. He answered her ring personally. He was a narrow-bodied man of medium height, thin brown hair razored away above the ears in the New York New Wave style. He wore wire-rim glasses on his beaklike nose. He also wore an old brown sweater and enormous baggy tan trousers from the 1940's—a look intended to be so deliberately old-fashioned it was chic.

He frowned at Sullivan, but said, "Hi, Bonnie. Come in."

They came in. He locked the door behind them, then took their coats and carefully hung them over his bathtub.

He came back into the living room. "Terry, this is Jack Sullivan. Jack, Terry Moreland." They shook hands. Moreland's hand was cold and soft. The apartment had a schizophrenic quality. The furniture was antique but the decorations were all modern art. Painfully modern. Sullivan looked at a combination painting and sculpture on the wall made of paint splashes and strips of curled black plastic and bottle caps glued onto canvas. Here and there the artist had deliberately ripped the canvas.

"The vandals do this too?" Sullivan asked, keeping a straight face.

Moreland raised an eyebrow and looked at Terry. "Is he serious?"

"No." She sat on the couch. Sullivan looked at the couch. It looked fragile. He decided to stand. Sullivan was big. He was more than six feet, more than two hundred pounds, most of it muscle. Staring at Sullivan, he looked at the scar on Sullivan's right cheek, at another scar bisecting his left eyebrow. The eyes, a blue that changed tint, could be dusty blue or the color of gunmetal when Sullivan was mad. . . .

"What exactly does Mr. Sullivan normally do for a living?" Moreland asked, looking at the gun in Sullivan's shoulder harness.

"What's it matter?" Sullivan said. "You need help. I can help. Bonnie knows me. You trust her?"

"Yes."

"She can vouch for me."

Bonnie nodded. "Jack is . . . a sort of bodyguard," she said.

Moreland crossed his arms and squirmed a little. His mouth was pinched. He started at a knock on the door.

"I'm sorry, Bonnie," Moreland said, "but I really need to know more about him, if he's going to work for us."

"I'm not going to work for you," Sullivan said. "But I'll work with you. I'm doing this gratis, for Bonnie. You couldn't afford my usual rates."

"I really must know," Moreland pressed. "We have to be careful when we are fighting a man like Legion. He might . . . well, he might hire people to infiltrate."

"What do *you* do, Moreland?" Sullivan asked. "For a living."

"I'm a free-lance curator."

Sullivan looked at him blankly.

"He curates for art galleries," Bonnie said. "Selects the artwork—"

"I know what a curator is," Sullivan said. "I was just

wondering why his profession made him an expert on dealing with guys like Legion."

"Terry organized the building security force," Bonnie pointed out.

"Why hasn't the building security force evicted the vandals, the goons, from those two apartments downstairs?"

"Well, we're not stormtroopers!" Moreland said. "We don't have the legal right—"

"They're threatening your safety. You have a right to defend yourself," Sullivan said. "Kick them out. They're not likely to go to the police. Neither is your crooked landlord."

"We are defending ourselves, our way. With lawyers. We're going to the root of the trouble."

"But meanwhile," Sullivan said. "They—"

He was interrupted by a banging on the door. Moreland crossed the room and shouted, "Who is it?"

"It's Jane, Terry!"

He unlocked the door and let her in. She was a tall black woman in designer jeans and a turtleneck sweater. Her hair had been straightened very professionally and she looked like a model in *Ebony*. Sullivan smiled and nodded at her. She looked out of breath and flustered as she turned to Moreland. "Terry, they're hassling Mr. Berrigan again."

"Oh God. Use my phone, call the police." Moreland went to his closet and took a can of Mace from it.

Sullivan started toward the door.

"We'll do this my way, Sullivan!" Moreland said, scurrying ahead of him, out into the hall.

Moreland pounded down the steps, shouting, "Eric! Eric!"

A man with freckles and thinning red hair came out onto the stairs a flight down. "Yeah?"

"Come on, they're at it again!"

Eric swore and came with him. Sullivan and Bonnie followed.

When they reached the bottom flight, Moreland and

Eric ran ahead and around the railing post to confront the three men under the stairs. Sullivan put a hand on Bonnie's arm, restraining her just beneath the top of the first flight, where they were above the attackers.

The three thugs had cornered a little white-haired man with a red face and a green vest. One of them had a gold watch with a piece of the vest material still attached to its chain. Looked like they'd ripped it out of the vest. They pushed and taunted the old man, shoving him against the wall.

Old Berrigan snarled back at them, "You slimy bastuds, I ain't scareda you! Come at me one at a time and I'll take you all on!" He raised his fists.

Sullivan smiled.

Moreland and Eric, breathless, halted a few steps from the three men and Moreland shouted, "Leave him alone or you'll get a face full of this!"

He raised a can of Mace.

The attackers were two Puerto Ricans and a gap-toothed Caucasian; all three were in their mid-twenties. The Hispanics were carefully if garishly groomed; the Caucasian had stringy, greasy hair and a ratty motorcycle jacket.

"Fuck you, man!" Jacket said. He grabbed the old man and pulled him in front of him, crooking an arm around Berrigan's neck. "You going to Mace the old fart too?"

"You . . . you let him go!" Eric said uncertainly. "The cops are coming."

"Bullshit they are," the taller of the two Hispanics said. He reached behind him and drew a knife. The other one pocketed the watch, and took a blackjack from his jacket.

"I'm warning you!" Moreland said.

"Christ," Sullivan muttered. And he vaulted over the stair railing.

He came down on his feet behind the two Spanish guys; before he hit the floor he hit the punks, slamming them each in the back of the neck with the heels of his hands, the momentum of his fall increasing the impact of the blows. Both goons went staggering across the hall, bounced on the opposite wall, and fell on their asses. Sullivan was up and moving at the white guy before he could do anything more than say, "What the fuck—"

Sullivan clamped a hand on the guy's wrist, pried it away from the old man, and said, "If you'll excuse us, Mr. Berrigan," as he twisted the punk's arm behind his back. The old man moved out of the way as Sullivan slammed the goon against the wall. Twice. Then he threw him aside like a man tossing a bag of garbage into a can. The goon went to his knees, spitting out his few teeth.

One of the Hispanics ran for the door. The one with the knife was up now, and he turned and slashed at Sullivan. Sullivan sidestepped, caught the knife arm and wrenched it expertly, dislocating the man's elbow. The thug screamed and dropped the knife. Sullivan rabbit-punched him in the chin. The thug's mouth clacked shut on the scream and he bit off the tip of his tongue. Sullivan grabbed him by the hair and the seat of the pants and ran him, bouncer-style, out the front door. He threw him headfirst out into the rain. He tumbled head over heel down the steps.

Sullivan went back and dragged the bloody-mouthed white guy to his feet by the collar. He shook him.

"Hey, man, come on, don't!" the guy squealed.

"You live here, asshole?" Sullivan asked through gritted teeth.

"No, no, man!"

"He's lying!" Berrigan said. "I seen him before with them others going in that apartment right there!"

"Who hired you?" Sullivan demanded.

"Nobody, man!"

Sullivan slammed him against the wall. Three times, hard. Plaster sifted down from the ceiling.

"Bonnie!" Moreland yelled. "Stop him! We could be sued for excessive use of force!"

"The hell with stopping him!" Berrigan said, picking up his watch from the floor. "They deserve every bit of it!"

"Berrigan's right," Eric said. "This guy's got the right idea."

Sullivan slammed the punk a fourth time against the wall. He groaned and said, "Crackwell! Crackwell got the place, told us what to do!"

Sullivan pulled the thug close and hissed in his ear, "You tell Crackwell there's a professional working here now. We'll tolerate no more of this crap."

He dragged the punk to the door and pitched him down the stairs.

"I wash my hands of this!" Moreland said thickly. "I'm not legally responsible for this!"

"Fine," Sullivan said. "I'm working independently. I'll take responsibility."

The stereo still blasted from the apartment Berrigan had indicated as belonging to the thugs.

Sullivan went to the door and kicked it in.

Eric gasped. Berrigan cackled with glee. Moreland groaned. Bonnie said, "Don't kill 'em, Jack!"

Sullivan had worked up a head of steam. He nodded briefly and stepped into the apartment.

Four shocked faces stared up at him from the floor to the right. They were sitting in a ring on the floor, smoking pot. One of them had a syringe and a spoon and a glass of water. Two white, two black.

"Crackwell believes in equal-opportunity hiring," Sullivan said. "That's nice." He crossed to the stereo beside the window. The gate over the window had been folded back. Sullivan picked up the portable cassette player—a big silvery one about three feet long and a foot thick—and threw it through the glass of the window. It smashed outside on the sidewalk.

"Hey, what the fuck!" One of the black guys yelled, standing.

"That was your friend's line a few minutes ago," Sullivan said. "You guys ought to get them straight."

Then he sucker-punched the guy in the Adam's apple. He went over backward, gagging. The others leapt to their feet.

Sullivan drew the gun.

"You need a warrant to come in here like this, man! You got a warrant?" a shaggy Caucasian demanded.

Sullivan laughed. "I ain't a cop, man," he said, mocking the tone a man uses when talking to the simple-minded. "I'm a tenant. And I don't want scumbags here hassling the other tenants and fucking up the place with graffiti. And putting holes in the wall. And setting fires. And making threats."

"You don't know who you're fucking with," the other black guy said. His companion was still wheezing.

Sullivan looked around. The apartment was empty. The refrigerator and stove were gone. "Looks like I'm dealing with lowlifes who steal refrigerators and stoves and sell them for dope money, among other things. Steal them right out of their own apartments."

"You racist cracker—" the black man began.

Sullivan pointed the gun at him and said, "Shut up." The guy shut up. Sullivan went on, " 'Racist' is a bad insult. I take it seriously. I don't like racists. I'll have to kick your ass if you call me that again. I'll tell you what I'm prejudiced against: junkies and thieves. Whatever their color. Now, the whole bunch of you: get the fuck out of here and don't ever come back."

"If you weren't holding that gun . . ." the black guy said.

Sullivan said, "You think I need this? Any of you guys carrying a piece?" They stared at him in response. "Turn around, put your hands on the wall," Sullivan said. "Spread your legs and arms, put your weight on your arms. Move!"

Grumbling, they did as he asked.

"Jack," Bonnie said from the door, "you need some backup?"

He shook his head. "Just watch to see if the cops come."

He patted the four punks down. He confiscated dope, pot, rolling papers, syringes, two small pistols, and four knives. He opened the heroin packages and dumped the powder on the floor, ground it into the board-cracks with his boot heel. The junkies groaned. He tossed the bags of pot out the window. The wind caught them and whipped them away. The pot-heads cursed behind him.

Then Sullivan put the knives and guns into Bonnie's care. He laid his own gun in the middle of the floor.

He stepped back and said, "Okay, turn around."

The four thugs turned to face him. They stared in surprise at the .44 Automag on the floor.

Sullivan spread his hands. "Look, Mom. No gun."

They gaped at him, then looked uncertainly at one another.

He said, "I want to teach you a lesson. So you know not to come around here, ever again. Show you you're just plain outclassed. And you can tell your friends. So come on. Go for the gun. Or go for me. Jump me. And we'll see if I need that piece."

"He be one big motherfucker," said the guy Sullivan had slugged. Hoarsely.

"He just one guy," said his friend. "We're four."

"Let's take him," said the shaggy white guy.

The other white guy was lean and wiry-looking. He grinned, showing a lot of mottled pink gum. His eyes were rimmed with red. "Let's kill the motherfucker."

He and the bigger black guy rushed Sullivan first. Their friends were a split second behind.

The shaggy white guy was bending to grab for the Automag. Sullivan stepped between them and the gun, and fiercely drop-kicked the shaggy punk in the teeth.

The bigger black made a grab for Sullivan's leg as he made the kick. But Sullivan twisted away, pivoted on his other foot, came around like a man completing a dance move, and kicked the nearest man—the lean one, lunging at him—in the gut. The man folded up. Sullivan slammed him in the jaw with his knee, at the same time swinging a right-handed haymaker at the big black guy, catching him hard on the side of the head. He staggered. The shorter one was coming at Sullivan from the right side, jabbing at his neck. Sullivan bunched the muscles in his neck at the last split second, taking the blow, then snapping his right arm back to slam the guy in the ribs under an armpit, in a sensitive nerve cluster. The thug yelped and stumbled back. Sullivan was already dealing with another. The black guy was coming from Sullivan's left, jabbing at his eyes while the white one tried to tackle him around the middle. Sullivan blocked the jab with his left arm and at the same moment brought his right fist down hard on the top of the tackler's head.

The Specialist's right knee came up to meet his own arm coming down, but there was something in the way. The tackler's head. Sullivan caught the guy's head between his fist and his knee, cracking his jaw like a walnut in a nutcracker. The guy screamed and jerked away, clutching at his broken jaw.

The black guy was swinging from another angle. Sullivan had to take a rabbit punch to the ribs. It hurt, but nothing broke. He countered with a right hook to the man's nose, followed up with a left jab, another right hook to the cheekbone, a left uppercut to the point of the chin, and then the big black guy was on his back, out cold.

The other black guy had since cut and run. The white guys were both crawling across the floor toward the door, both holding shattered jaws.

"You guys beginning to get the message?" Sullivan asked.

The cops never did show. An hour after the men had left—two walking, one carried—the police still hadn't answered Jane's phone call.

Sullivan spoke to her in Moreland's living room.

"You dial 911?" he asked.

She shook her head. "Maybe I should've. But there was a cop here said if we had any trouble with this goon squad we should call a Detective Krinsky. So I called Krinsky. He said he'd send some guys to look into it."

Sullivan looked at Bonnie, who was sitting on the couch beside Moreland. "You got anything on this Krinsky?"

She shook her head. "But could be he's on Legion's payroll."

Sullivan nodded. "That's the way I figure it."

"What do we do now?" Moreland asked. He had accepted Sullivan's authority.

"Any more assholes on Legion's payroll in the building?" Sullivan asked.

Moreland mused, "There's another apartment they use sometimes. Usually they're not in it. They don't seem to be now. Sometimes they have parties. Bring in girls, and some men who I think are the girls' tricks."

"They do a prostitution thing there sometimes . . ." Sullivan said. "Okay. We'll wait for that to crop up and deal with it when it comes. Right now, I'd better check out my new apartment."

Moreland had the keys ready. He took Sullivan down a floor and opened the door to number 3B. It was a studio apartment, renovated but small, furnished with a fold-out couch, a kitchen table, two chairs, and basic appliances. "I'll take it," Sullivan said. Moreland gave him the keys.

"We're having a meeting at nine tomorrow morning, Mr. Sullivan. My place. All the tenants will be there."

Sullivan nodded and said, "Me too." Moreland left.

Sullivan looked at Bonnie. "How do you feel? Any headache? Dizziness?"

"Nope." She sat down on the couch. "But I'm worried. About those bodies."

"I'll take care of it tonight." He'd hidden the bodies he'd left in her office building in an empty room down the hall from hers. "The weather's supposed to break tomorrow. So tonight I'll bury the bodies in that construction site, where they're going to put in the sidewalk. Looked to me like they'll put the concrete for the sidewalk down soon as the weather makes it possible. . . . Somebody sure timed that construction badly."

"There was a construction workers' strike while you were out of town."

"That's what I like about you, the sexy conversation."

"You don't think you're gong to seduce me again!"

"Me! Seduce *you!*" He snorted. Then, from the look on her face, he realized he was taking the wrong tack. "Well, I was hoping to, yeah, can't blame a guy for thinking about something real good and wanting that something real good to happen again."

He sat down beside her.

"Was it really good?"

"Think back. You'll remember. No, don't bother. I'll remind you."

He put his arms around her.

The shrill laughter from the hallway woke him at three in the morning. He sat up and looked at Bonnie. She was still asleep. He slipped carefully off the couch-bed and, quietly as he could, got into his clothes. He went to the window, softly opened it, and listened. More laughter and music. Sounded like it was coming from one of the first-floor apartments. The one that was sometimes used as a brothel. He put the Automag in his holster and went out onto the fire escape. It was slick with dampness, but the rain had stopped. The fire escape creaked and its bolts grated in their sockets as he climbed down to the first floor. A siren wailed in the night. The wind soughed through the iron of the fire escape. The disco throb rose as he got lower.

He climbed down the ladder and looked in the window of the first-floor apartment. The shades were down but he was high enough to peer over the top of the shades' roller. This apartment was across the hall from the room Sullivan had rousted that afternoon. It had a bed and a couch, and not much else. There were two women and two men in the room; one couple on the couch, one on the bed. As Sullivan watched, feeling like a voyeur and not liking the feeling, two men came in the room from the kitchen and went to the door to the hall.

Sullivan climbed down the ladder and dropped to the sidewalk. He heard a startled squeak and looked up to see Jane, coming home from her cocktail-waitress job. She wore a raincoat and carried an umbrella under her arm. And she was staring at Sullivan. "What you doing on the fire escape?" she asked. "There a fire?"

He smiled and shook his head. "I'm just doing a little . . . patrol. Go on in and go home."

She went inside. At the same moment, Sullivan heard the hall door open. He frowned.

Marv Bixter was having a good time. It seemed Tony's contacts were just as good as he'd claimed. He'd got them both a couple of girls, a safe place to take them, and a gram of coke apiece, all for six hundred bucks. Even threw in a fifth of Jack Daniel's.

"This is like one of those what you call your Club Med deals, Tony," Marv said, smoking a cigarette as the girl's head bobbed over his open fly. "This is what you call your all-inclusive travel package."

Tony answered with a grunt. He was on the bed, pumping away into the other girl. A Spanish girl in a blond wig. Marv's was a redhead with large angular cheekbones. She hadn't yet taken off her dress. She seemed a little reluctant about that. There was something funny about the girl, but Marv couldn't quite place it. Still, she did a good job. Funny how wide her shoulders were. . . .

Marv was reaching for his cocaine when it hit him. "Hey, wait a minnut!" he said, jerking his member from her mouth. It came out with a cork-popping sound. "Hey, Tony, I think this one's a drag queen!"

"Well, honey, what did you expect from a discount travel package?" the transsexual said, putting his hands on his hips.

"Well, mine's real!" Tony said.

"Of course she is!" the redhead pouted. "*She* had someone to pay for her sex change!"

"Sex change!" Tony yelped, sitting up.

The redhead was wriggling against Marv like a cat searching for someone to pet it. Now that he looked at her more closely, he could see a little stubble on her chin through the makeup. The transsexual adjusted one of his silicon breasts in its brassiere and whined, "Marvy, why don't *you* pay for my sex change? I'd be your little girl forever and ever if you'd—"

"Get offa me, goddammit!" Marv shouted.

That's when the two Puerto Rican guys who'd sold them this deal came into the room from the hall, pushing a black girl ahead of them. The two guys were named Julio and Manuel. One had a mustache and a Che Guevara beret; the other had a small pointed beard and a Fidel Castro cap. Neither one was Communist, they just liked the look.

They were drunk and stoned, too. "Look what we found in the hall. Now we got some pussy for us too!" Manuel cackled, shoving Jane further into the room.

"Hey, what's the deal with these here drag queens!" Tony said, getting out of the bed and tugging on his pants. "We was supposed to have real girls! I want my money back!"

But Marv was staring at the hall door. There was a man standing there behind Manuel and Julio. He was a big man with a scarred face and a big gun in his hand. A *big* gun.

"You shouldn't have taken the drugs and drunk so much," the man in the doorway said. "Or you'd have noticed before that the girls weren't girls. Now, grab your stuff and leave."

The transsexuals pulled on their coats and ran out, carrying their purses and shoes in their arms.

"Who the fuck are you?" Manuel demanded. He was standing behind Jane, holding her arm twisted behind her back.

Julio drew a knife. The big gun in the stranger's hand

thundered once, and the knife flew from Julio's hand. Julio swore and sucked the fingers stung by the impact of the slug on the knife blade.

"I could have put that slug through your head," the scar-faced guy said. He turned to Marv and Tony. "Get the fuck out of here. Never come back."

Marv reached for his cocaine. Scarface said, "Leave it here, it's going into the toilet."

Tony scurried into his clothes as Marv zipped up his trousers and they grabbed their coats. The big guy stood aside so they could leave. A moment later they were out on the sidewalk, under the window of the apartment they'd just left. It was beginning to drizzle.

Marv was pissed. "I say we go in there and club that bastard," he said, taking a blackjack from his coat. "He's in the door with his back to the hall. We paid for those drugs and we should have them!"

"I don't know, Marv," Tony said. "He's an awful big, mean-looking guy. And he's got that gun."

"Didn't you see? When we went out I looked back and he was putting the gun in its holster! I say we go up there and—"

He broke off, interrupted by the sound of breaking glass. Julio came flying out the window, thrown bodily through the glass to fall on his face on the sidewalk. "Oh shit-man-motherfucker!" he whined, on his hands and knees, his nose bloody.

There was a scream, and then Manuel came flying through the window, bringing what was left of the glass with him. He fell at Tony's feet.

"Uh . . . maybe you're right," Marv said, backing away from the fallen men. "Maybe you're right, Tony. Let's not go in there. . . . Tony. . . ?"

Tony was already halfway down the block.

4

Jack Sullivan: Target

Legion sat at his desk, polishing his eye.

Crackwell didn't like it when Legion took the glass eye out of its socket. It made him nauseous—especially to see that empty left eye socket. But he didn't dare say anything about it. Legion had a bad temper.

It was eight A.M. A gray morning at Legion's house in Queens, New York, and Legion sat in his office polishing his glass eye with a special cloth.

"How many, did you say?" Legion asked. He was a barrel-shaped man with graying hair dyed blond, the dye fading to show the gray in spots now, and a long reddish face with bags under his smoky blue eyes—the real one and the glass one.

"Eight guys, one after another. We think it's the same guy who did the bums we sent to rough up the girl."

"You really think he burned those guys? Nobody found bodies."

Crackwell shrugged. He was an ex-cop, forced to retire ten years early to avoid charges of taking protection money. He had thick brown hair, a nose that looked as if it had been broken at least twice, and a droopy mustache that went with his equally droopy brown eyes. He wore a three-piece gray pinstripe suit.

He liked to look like an executive. "After last night I think so, yeah."

Legion nodded. "What you doing about it?"

Crackwell looked at his watch. "I sent two guys over there an hour ago with an offer. We pay him ten thou if he lays off and we get back to work clearing out that building. But you know something, boss, I'm beginning to think that building ain't worth the trouble. You got plenty of other holdings. We could sell it to the tenants—"

Legion banged a meaty fist down on the desk. The glass eye on the desktop leapt like an aggressive snail. "It's the principle! That building is mine! Whatever's mine I do what I want with! You get me? I won't be defied by a bunch of candyasses who've hired themselves a detective and some fucking ex-marine!"

"I know how you feel," Crackwell soothed, as Legion put his eye back in. "It's just that this guy seems like he might be a real pro. He sent a message about it, saying he was a pro. He acts like a pro—"

"So if he's a pro, he'll take a fee to back off. Pros work for money."

The front doorbell rang.

"Go see what that is, will you, Crackwell?" Legion said, adjusting his eye in its socket with a hand mirror.

Crackwell nodded and went out. He went to the front door and opened it. There was no one out there.

But he was wrong, they just weren't standing on the step. They were lying at his feet. It was the two guys he'd sent to buy out the pro. They were lying on the front steps, trussed hand and foot in a rope. They were bruised about the face, and one had a split lip. Whoever had left them had tied them together back to back. They wriggled and made muffled noises of outrage through their gags.

Crackwell swore, and dragged them into the hall before the neighbors could see them. There was a piece of paper tucked under one of the ropes. Crackwell pulled it out and looked at it. The note said:

Found your stray dogs. If they stray into my territory again I will kill them and then I'll hunt down the rest of their pack. Sell the building to a reputable landlord. This is your last warning.

The Specialist.

"The Specialist," Crackwell muttered. "Great."

He turned away, started back to the office. The two men whined through their gags, demanding to be cut loose. Crackwell said, "I'll let you loose when I'm good and ready, you stumblebum fuck-ups!" He hurried to Legion's office. "Boss, I want to show you something. Out in the hall."

Legion scowled but got up and followed. Crackwell showed him the two trussed thugs, and the note.

"What the hell is this?" Legion demanded. "Who's 'the Specialist'?"

"A pro. A . . . kind of mercenary. A hit artist. But—"

"So okay, he's high-priced, and we didn't offer him enough money. We'll double it."

"You don't understand, boss. I didn't know it was the Specialist or I wouldn't have wasted my time offering money. He works for money sometimes, but he's weird. He only works if it's like, you know, a 'cause.' Something he believes in. Truth, justice, and the American way. Thinks he's Batman maybe. He's a specialist at taking vengeance—but only against people who really deserve it. That's the legend, anyway."

"Legend is right! Probably not even him. Just a trick to scare us. I read about this Specialist bullshit, I remember it now. It's a lot of hokum. The guy doesn't exist. Or if he does, they exaggerate the hell out of what he does! No one guy could've done that stuff!"

Crackwell sighed and shook his head. "When I was on the force we heard—"

"When you were on the force! I'm sick of hearing about that!"

"Listen, boss, there was an APB out for this guy. He's real. And no way he's going to take money. Shit, they've lost count of how many men he's supposed to have killed."

"I say it's bullshit. Okay, he exists, but the legend is all exaggeration."

"Maybe."

"Maybe my ass! Hire ten new men and get the bastard out of there! Tell them to shoot him if they have to, but get him out! And see that they keep the pressure up on those tenants! I want them out! Matter of principle!" The hall echoed with his words. He strode to the men tied up on the rug and kicked them viciously in the ribs. "Fuck-ups!" he screamed.

At that moment, Jack Sullivan was at the tenants' meeting in Moreland's apartment. Eighteen people had shown, eight women and ten men. Bonnie and Jane and Moreland sat on the couch. The others sat in kitchen chairs or folding chairs placed in a semicircle. Sullivan stood at the opening of the circle. He'd listened to their ideas and opinions and complaints for an hour. Now he had something to say.

"Legion's a bad guy all right," he said, "but I don't think you know *how* bad. Sure, he was listed by the *Village Voice* as one of the ten worst landlords in New York. Sure, he'll let tenants go months without a furnace in the winter, so that some die of hypothermia. Right, he doesn't maintain the places, and if you complain, or if he wants you out before your lease is up so he can sell the place, he'll send goons around to terrorize you out. But that's just the beginning. Bonnie's found out he's involved in heroin trafficking. I can tell you from experience that men in the drug trade murder as casually as a farmer slaughters a lamb. The guy may well be willing to kill. Chances are he's done it before."

"Why are you telling us this, Sullivan?" Moreland asked.

"Because I want you to know what you're up against. How serious it is. And that should tell you what you're going to have to do about it. You'll have to fight. How many here besides Bonnie have a gun or a gun permit?"

No one raised their hand. Sullivan went on, "How many are willing to fight? I mean, *physically* fight."

Five of the men and two of the women raised their hands. Sullivan looked at the women who'd volunteered. They were short-haired dykes wearing blue jeans and plaid shirts. "Both of us take martial arts," said the one wearing thick glasses.

"Trouble with martial-arts courses, they don't really give you practical training on how to apply what you learn. They teach it as if it's a sport, which it is. But most people who've studied karate or the other martial arts have trouble when it comes to actually using them against someone in a fighting situation. A lot of that trouble is psychological. You've got to be willing to kick someone's face off."

"Oh, we're willing all right," said the bespectacled dyke grimly.

"Good. Now, I can't ask anyone here to carry a gun. The cops find you with those and without a permit, you go to prison for two years in this state. But we can outfit you with some other goodies." From a leather case at his feet he took something that looked like a hydraulic shock absorber. It was about a foot and a half long and made of black-painted steel. "This is a Prowler Fouler," Sullivan said. "Also called an impact gun. It shoots a bag filled with buckshot at a very high speed. It punches the guy out for you. He'll feel like Muhammad Ali gave him a medium-strength right cross. Stun him good, but won't hurt him badly. You drop the bag in this end, crank the spring at this end, and fire by turning this ring." He fired the impact gun at the floor. The pouch rebounded with an audible thump.

In her place on the couch, Jane jumped a little at the noise. Sullivan looked at her. She knotted her hands nervously in her lap and stood up, and turned to the others. "I'm sorry—I can't handle this. Those guys grabbed me and almost raped me last night. I hate violence. I can't . . . I can't deal with it. I'm moving out." Some of the tenants tried to argue with her. But she left, two others following closely behind her.

Sullivan shrugged and said, "Let's get back to the demonstration, for those of you planning to stick it out."

"I'm staying," old Berrigan said. "I've been here thirty years and I'll be damned if some rat's asshole is gonna chase me out!"

The others cheered at that. Sullivan smiled, and gave Berrigan an impact gun.

"Now, this," Sullivan said, taking a big silvery tube from the bag, "is a 35,000-candlepower flashlight, the Stream Light 35. Shine this directly in the guy's eyes and he'll be temporarily blinded or confused. Also makes a good club. I've got three of these. Here are a couple of nightsticks, which are pretty self-explanatory. . . . Here are two pellet guns. Won't kill them but can blind them, distract them, make them stop and think twice. I'll show you how to make some effective weapons out of car antennas, and a few items one can find around the house. Here we have two tactical radios. They clip to the belt and you listen on them and speak into them via this headset. You should have it with you at all times when you are in the building, especially at night. They have a range of a mile. Use nine-volt DC batteries. These models are voice-actuated. We'll have to get some more, one for everyone. If anyone is attacked or sees anything strange going on, they should call the others on the defense team with these."

"What about Mace?" Moreland asked.

"The stuff is a bit dangerous to use because you have to get close to the assailant to ensure its effectiveness, and if you're outside, the wind just might turn it against you. In the right situation it can be useful. You might prefer this." He drew a big black gun from his case. "This is a gun that fires tear-gas capsules. As you can see, it's designed to look like a regular gun. Threaten them with the gun and they'll think it shoots regular bullets. If they attack anyway or if there's no time to bluff them, fire the pellet at the assailant's chest. It will explode and flood his face with tear gas. Should incapacitate him for a few minutes. If worse comes to worst, you have kitchen knives. You can buy fighting knives. And you might consider carrying a small bag of fine-ground black pepper in your pocket or purse. Fling a cloud of pepper in his eyes—it's just as good as tear gas or Mace."

"You keep talking as if the assailant has to be a *he!*" objected the spectacled dyke. "That's sexism! Women can be dangerous criminals too!"

"Be sure to have that included as a clause in the Equal Rights Amendment," Sullivan said. "Now, as it's not raining outside, let's go up to the roof, where I'll demonstrate some of these things and some simple self-defense moves."

The tenants had taken a day off work to prepare for the defense of their home. They spent most of the day in training. At nightfall it began to rain and they went inside.

Sullivan and Bonnie went downstairs to Sullivan's apartment for dinner. The previous tenant had left hastily and the phone was still connected. Sullivan used it to order pizza and meatball heroes from a joint on the corner. Bonnie went out for beer, wearing the tactical radio headset in case she were attacked. When she came back, Sullivan was laying their dinner out on the table. She turned on a portable radio and they listened to an FM station play a Beatles retrospective.

"You know, it's kind of nice and cozy with you here," she said, after drinking a couple of beers spiked with some of Sullivan's whiskey. "A girl could get used to it."

Sullivan didn't say anything. He thought sadly of the two women who had died from being too close to him. There was nothing he'd like more than settling down with Bonnie somewhere. But it just wasn't in the cards. It was too dangerous for the woman.

Bonnie took his silence as indifference. She cleaned up the scraps of dinner and then went to stare moodily out the window.

"You know, we could avoid all this business of preparing for a siege," Sullivan said, "if you gave me the go-ahead to burn him."

"It wouldn't be right, Jack, dammit!" she said.

He shrugged, wondering why she was so snappish.

The night wore on and the whiskey ran low.

Feeling himself a shade drunk, Sullivan decided he'd better move around and burn the alcohol tipsiness off. "I'm going to check out the roof," he said. "I've got a hunch about it."

She shrugged as if she didn't care what he did. He put on his short leather jacket. It covered the Automag in its shoulder holster. He clipped a small flashlight onto his belt and went out onto the stairs and up to the deserted roof. Although it was quiet, he somehow felt that the roof was the next place the attack would come from.

The building was flanked by two others, the one on the east side slightly taller, the other a few feet shorter. Sullivan prowled the three rooftops and saw no one. Behind his building was an airshaft and there was a pigeon coop on the higher building. The pigeons made soft cooing noises as he passed them, fluttering once or twice as they noticed him. On the far side of the eastern building he found a narrow alley, with a fire escape running up from it. That'd be a good entry point for them.

He went back to his own building and sat in the deep shadow behind the elevator-motor housing. He squatted with his back to the tin wall, looking east.

He'd done something like this a few dozen times in Vietnam. You look for the most likely place the enemy will pick as its attack point. You set up a blind there, or simply station yourself out of direct line of sight. You watch the spot. You wait. Nine times out of ten, nothing happens.

But that tenth time . . .

So Sullivan waited. The whiskey wore off and the chill began to seep into him. He wanted a cigarette, but if he lit one and the enemy happened to be around, they'd see the match flare.

The city droned to itself. A statistician's graph line of lights lit up the skyline. Below in the street, someone honked a trick car horn that played shave-and-a-haircut-two-bits. And then he tensed.

The pigeons were fluttering in their coop. Something was disturbing them.

Someone was coming over the rooftop. He reached into his coat for the gun—and then withdrew his hand empty. Don't litter the streets with bodies this time, Bonnie had said. The tenants could get in trouble if they were implicated. He couldn't kill the guys and explain to the cops why he'd had to do it—he was still officially a wanted man. They weren't actively looking for him, but if he just happened to turn up on their porch, arms full of corpses, they'd bust him all right.

Unless these assholes forced his hand, he would kill them somewhere far from this building. Which meant he was going to have to take these guys out non-lethally. . . .

This time.

5

The Velvet Glove in the Iron Fist

Trouble is, Sullivan thought, watching the men move across the adjacent roof, *there's five of them and they're all carrying guns*.

Question: How was he going to neutralize five guys carrying pistols and submachine guns, without using his own weapon—and without getting himself offed trying?

Answer: Very carefully.

The five men were wearing ski masks. The two in front carried small Skorpion submachine guns. The three behind in single file carried pistols.

They hadn't spotted Sullivan. They were moving along the front of the buildings; he was hiding near the back.

Sullivan moved to the rear of the elevator-motor housing, a small outbuilding that also contained the entrance to the stairs leading downward.

He found what he was looking for: a TV antenna wire. He wrapped the wire around his fist near the antenna and jerked it free. Somewhere below, *Dallas* abruptly got snowy on someone's set.

On the roof, Sullivan took a knife from his boot and cut the wire where it dropped over the edge of the roof. That gave him a coil about twenty feet long.

Sullivan wrapped it around his arm and carried it into the outbuilding.

The door was on the east side; the five marauders were coming from the west so they didn't see him go in. But they'd be here soon—he had to move fast.

Four steps down from the topmost flight, Sullivan found a crack between the iron strip edging the step and the concrete of the step itself. He wedged one end of the wire into it, then threw the other end over the banister. It looped to the stairwell to hang below. He slackened it and then crimped it, so the wire ran across the step, up a banister post, and over the rail. The stairway was dim. With luck they wouldn't notice it. He went quickly down another flight and pressed himself against the wall, holding one end of the wire but careful not to pull it in the slightest.

Directly overhead, the door opened. Sullivan heard the tramp of feet. Men walking down the stairs. He counted the steps. The first one passed. Second, third. Number four was coming. In a moment, the first would turn the corner and see Sullivan below.

The fifth was just stepping over the stair Sullivan had booby-trapped.

The Specialist jerked hard on the line.

Above, the line went taut across the stairway, right between the fifth marauder's legs. He shouted and pitched forward, tumbling down the stairs atop the fourth, knocking the fourth into the third, and the third into the second, all four men falling head over heels into one another. The first turned the corner.

Sullivan had the .44 out, holding it at arm's length and sighting carefully at the dim outline of the submachinegun in the man's hands. The man spotted Sullivan and raised the gun in his hands, preparing to fire.

Sullivan squeezed off a single round. The big gun bucked in his hand and the slug went precisely home, knocking the Skorpion from the gunman's hands.

The man shouted and staggered back, thrusting his

hands into his armpits—hands stung by his own "scorpion." Sullivan moved in, just as two of the others on the stairs were getting to their feet and raising their guns.

Sullivan transferred the gun to his left hand, put his right foot up on the side of a stair on the flight above, grabbed the rail with his right hand, and with a heave that twisted some muscles in his arm and back, making him grunt with pain, he vaulted up and over the rail. His left foot went over first, struck a gun hand, knocking a .45 automatic from it, then came down on someone's leg. Then someone howled. The other leg swung over and Sullivan turned to face the men as soon as he had a foot planted. He completed the turn like a dance spin, kicking another gun away.

Someone threw a punch at him. He avoided the fist by twisting left, swacking the .44's barrel across the man's skull as he lashed out with his right fist, smashing another man back so he tumbled down the stairs once more, knocking two of his friends down the moment they'd gotten to their feet.

For five seconds there was a confused tangle of arms and legs and men struggling to get to their feet. Sullivan had a glimpse of the man whose gun he'd shot from his hands and who was now trying to get the Skorpion to work. But the shot had damaged it, and it was jammed. The other submachine-gunner was still trying to get out from under two other men. One of the men was out cold—Sullivan's right to his chin had smashed his head back against the wall. The fifth man had bent over and was grabbing for a gun lying at his feet. Sullivan grabbed him by the seat of his pants and his collar and pitched him over the railing. He fell wailing, dropping the gun, and flipped over to land on his back on the stairs below. He shouted and clutched at his back. He'd broken a shoulder blade.

Sullivan reached down and snatched up the gun. Then, a gun in each hand, he moved up a step and shouted, "Freeze, lunkheads, or I'll blast each one of you a new asshole!"

They froze, and Sullivan began the task of disarming and untangling them.

But Legion had sent ten men.

The other five were hitting the building from the front. Eric, coming home from the liquor store, spotted them getting out of two long black cars, pulling ski masks over their faces. Eric sprinted for the door, fumbled his key into the lock, and ran inside, shouting up the stairs.

Bonnie heard him. She grabbed her pistol, a .25, and an impact gun, and ran out into the hall, up the stairs, to bang on Moreland's door. There were two men from the building's security force in with Moreland, talking over strategy.

In the three minutes it took the goons to climb the steps and check the two apartments on the first floor— both empty—the tenants' security force deployed according to Sullivan's instructions.

Bonnie went down the fire escape with Eric. They came in the front door, coming up behind the hired hardmen. Moreland and Jim Cooper, another tenant, waited inside the apartment, pressed to either side of the door. The two dykes, Jay and Georgina, were on a landing a flight above. Berrigan had gone to the basement, where he threw a switch.

On the top floor, Sullivan had the five punks against the wall, hands pressed against it, lined up along the landing. When the old man threw the basement switch, the lights went out. Sullivan grabbed the flashlight on his belt and switched it on, holding the light in his left hand and the .44 in his right. The light shone on the five faces; the men had turned to come at him the instant the light went out. He grinned and fired at their feet, the rounds kicking up the chips of concrete. The five men moved back almost with the same motion.

"Turn the fuck around again," Sullivan said through clenched teeth.

They did what they were told.

Four flights down, the five other hardmen were bumbling into one another in the darkness, swearing.

"Where the hell are we?" one of them whispered.

"Shut up!" their leader shouted. "Didn't one of you bozos bring a flashlight?"

"Here's a flashlight for you!" Moreland shouted, throwing the door open and shining one of the 35,000-candlepower flashlights in their eyes.

The men yelled and covered their faces. Their leader cursed and raised his .45—but Cooper quickly fired an impact gun at his chest. The gun's pouch smacked into him with the impact of a chain-mailed karate punch and the guy went over backward, knocking one of his men down with him.

One of the other men raised his gun, squinting against the light. A voice cried out from above, "Up here!" As the men turned toward the sound, Jay and Georgina dumped two buckets of scalding ammoniated water on their faces. The men screamed, burned with heat and chemicals, blinded now for at least a few minutes. Below, Bonnie shouted to Berrigan, and he switched the lights back on.

Moreland and Cooper and the two dykes ran among the thugs, confiscating guns from the stumbling, swearing thugs, using nightsticks on any who resisted. Two of the men broke away and ran down the steps. Bonnie and Eric met the two toughs at the bottom; Eric fired a tear-gas gun at one while Bonnie knocked the other down with the impact gun. At the same time, Berrigan came up the stairs carrying rope as Moreland and Cooper, threatening the men with confiscated guns, herded them into the first-floor hallway.

On the top floor, Sullivan had tied each man's hands behind his back with wire. He ordered them down the stairs, followed along behind with the .44 out and ready.

He stopped, staring, when they got to the steps leading to the first-floor landing.

There were five other men lying on the hall floor, moaning, their hands tied behind their backs. Tenants stood around them, grinning up at him.

"Damn!" Sullivan blurted. "You people learn *fast!*"

The tenants cheered.

6
The Next Step . . .
Is Booby-trapped

"So what's the next step?" Moreland wondered aloud. "Do we or don't we?"

"Do we or don't we what?" Jay asked, pushing her thick glasses back on her formidable nose.

"Do we call the cops?"

"Of course we call the cops!" she hissed.

"But Sullivan and Bonnie think there's someone on Legion's payroll in the police department. He'd just let these creeps go."

Bonnie shook her head. "He couldn't do that. Not if we all sign complaints. These guys were carrying guns. They're going to jail."

They were in the basement. The ten men were sitting on the floor, their ski masks removed, looking miserable or defiant, depending on which one you looked at.

Sullivan stood to one side, a submachine gun in his hands. Now and then one of the men looked at the stairs, as if contemplating making a break for it. But then he'd look at the submachine gun and decide against it.

"Hey!" one of the thugs said. He was a black guy, probably not yet twenty. "I wasn't carrying no gun! I was just tryin' to earn a little extra cash! I got a sick mother!"

Sullivan snorted.

Two others spoke up, insisting they hadn't been carrying guns.

"I took note of which ones were," Moreland said. "You won't all be charged with that."

"Them three that was unarmed," Berrigan chimed in, "they was the vandals I saw in the hall tearin' up the floor and bustin' out the door that day!"

"Were they, now," Moreland said. "That's interesting. Now that we've got them where we want them, maybe we'll turn in the other seven and keep these three for our own personal punishment."

"What're you gonna do to us?" one of the men asked, wide-eyed.

"You're going to renovate the hall and the front door and the railings and the steps, and Mr. Berrigan needs someone to paint his apartment. We can stand shifts watching them."

The thugs groaned.

It made headlines. Bonnie managed to keep Sullivan out of the reports. There was no need for him to deal with the cops. There were more than enough tenants willing to sign complaints.

Four days passed, and Legion made no further moves. But neither did he send anyone around to do the repairs the tenants' attorney had asked for.

The three "prisoners"—who hadn't been mentioned to the cops—were hard at work painting, scrubbing, oiling, hammering, all under Eric's watchful eye. Berrigan assisted him, and both were armed with tear-gas guns which the three punks believed to be regular bullet-firing pistols. At night the thugs slept on cots in the basement, handcuffed to the pipes. "I'm a light sleeper," Berrigan warned them, "and I'm hoping I'll hear noises in the night that tell me you're trying to break loose down here, so I can come down and shoot you. Faith, what a pleasure that'll be!" There were no escape attempts.

Reporters came and went, and Sullivan avoided them; the other tenants were careful not to mention Sullivan's part in the capture. After the fifth day, the story died. It was replaced with "GRANDMA STRANGLES HUSBAND, BLAMES DEVIL."

A week after the assault, Sullivan, Moreland, and Bonnie met with the tenants' attorney, Harrison Winter, in Winter's office.

His office was the living room of his apartment. Framed certificates, shelves of lawbooks, and a big desk helped create the illusion that it was a real office. There was even a potted palm in one corner.

Winter was a big man with hairy arms who looked as if he should have gone into football instead of law. He had his law-school graduation ring on his right pinky, and he wore a gray vest over a light blue shirt, the sleeves rolled back from his immense, bristling forearms.

"Hi, come on in," the young attorney said, opening the door himself. "The secretary's off today."

Moreland chuckled, knowing that Winter had a secretary only one day a week.

They sat on a brown vinyl couch under a print of a photo of the country's first Supreme Court. Winter sat across from them, putting his hands together and lacing his fingers before saying, "The, uh, news isn't good."

Moreland frowned. "What happened?"

"Looks like there'll be no indictment against Legion for sending those goons out after you."

"But they had automatic weapons," Bonnie said. "And they admitted working for him!"

"They admitted working for Crackwell," Winter corrected. "And Crackwell works for Legion. But we can't prove Legion ordered it because Crackwell is legally autonomous from Legion."

"It's Legion's building," Sullivan growled.

Winter looked at him, appraising him. A V of concern showed on his forehead. He had pegged Sullivan as some kind of professional. "You—work for Bonnie here?"

"No. I'm just a concerned . . . tenant. I'm subletting

from someone in the building. My name's Stark. Richard Stark," Sullivan said.

Moreland glanced at Sullivan and raised an eyebrow, but said nothing.

Winter shrugged. "Doesn't matter that it's Legion's building. Crackwell's defense attorney claims the men belong to a gang that terrorizes the area and just happened to pick Legion's building. Their statements are probably going to be thrown out as evidence because they are supposed to have made them under death threats."

"Whose death threats?" Moreland demanded.

Winter cleared his throat in embarrassment. "Berrigan. He evidently told them they'd better talk and finger Crackwell and Legion or he'd personally castrate them and let them bleed to death."

"What! But he's just a blustering old man! He was telling them to tell the truth, that's all."

Winter went on, "It seems that one of the tenants, Jane Weston, was coming into the building to pick up some of her things—she was evidently moving out— when . . ." He looked at a sheaf of papers on his desk. "When she overheard Berrigan making his threats to the prisoners. One of the prisoners described her, and Officer Krinsky paid a visit and took her statement confirming the death threat."

"Krinsky again," Sullivan said coldly. "He's deliberately queering the investigation."

Winter shrugged again. "I'm inclined to agree with you. I think he threatened Ms. Weston in some way. But we can't prove that."

"What it boils down to," Bonnie said, "is that Legion and Crackwell are getting off scot-free."

Winter nodded. "Looks that way. At least those seven we put away are going to be put away for a while. Two years at least. Even if the extortion, burglary, and assault charges are dropped, they'll still have them for possession of illegal weapons and carrying handguns without a license."

"That's not good enough," Sullivan said. Something in his tone made everyone look at him.

"Jack . . ." Bonnie said warningly.

Winter looked at her. "I thought he said his name was Richard."

"Uh . . . Jack is a sort of nickname. It's his middle name and sometimes he goes by it."

Winter was studying Sullivan's face. "You look familiar. Have we met before?"

Sullivan shook his head. He knew where Winter had probably seen him before. The newspaper. Or maybe the photo of him that had been reproduced in *Time*, while he was being sought for slaughtering the Mafia don Toscani and a couple dozen of his men.

"What did you mean, Mr. . . . Stark," Winter went on, "when you said, 'That's not good enough'? What would you have me do?"

"Take it to the D.A. Or the Justice Department."

Winter sighed. "I have made a few inquiries in that direction. Evidently Legion is being investigated in some kind of covert operation. They're afraid if they push him on this, he'll run. If he leaves the country, they'll lose their operation. They've been setting it up for more than a year. They figure it'll take at least another year. Something to do with drug smuggling."

Bonnie said, "Legion owns a fleet of cargo planes. He may be using them to smuggle dope."

"That's even more reason he's got to be stopped," Sullivan said.

Winter looked sharply at him. "You're given to melo-dramatic statements, Mr. Stark."

Sullivan snorted. He got up and walked out.

He had plans to make.

7

Pro Versus Pro

Legion paced his office, smoking a cigar, sending up whirlpools of malodorous blue smoke. He glanced at his watch. Two-thirty. Damn that lawyer. What was he doing? Taking lunch at a time like this?

The phone rang.

Legion sprang for the receiver and bellowed, "Yeah?" into it.

"It's Seranno. How you doing, Mr. Legion—"

"Can the friendly bullshit and give!"

"We got it, Mr. Legion. They dropped the indictment."

Legion grinned. Amazing what you could do with a couple of lawyers and a fistful of hundred-dollar bills. A little greasing here, a little looping the loophole there, and you were home-free.

"Good work," Legion said, "but stay on top of it. I don't wanna hear no more about this."

"You can count on us, Mr. Legion. Well, how's the wife?"

"I haven't got a wife, you idiot!" Legion barked irritably, hanging up.

Crackwell came in. "Hey, boss, did you hear—"

"I just got the good news from Seranno. Now we're freed up to move against this asshole 'Specialist' guy."

"Look, boss, uh, I been doing some asking around. I

don't think we should mess with that guy anymore. I think you maybe oughta take a little vacation. The weather's getting cold. I think you oughta take a vacation where it's nice and warm. Mexico maybe."

"Okay, tell you what I'll do. I've gotta go to Sicily, to see Carola. I was supposed to go next month. I'll move it up, leave in a day or two. It's warmer there, and then again, it's not so warm, if you catch my meaning. I got to inspect the new crates, make sure the fucking camouflage is going to work. Jeez, the Feds got Frank Westroth trying to smuggle the stuff in, in furniture. Got to make sure we got it cop-proof and dog-sniffing proof."

"Sure, Sicily's fine. But stick there awhile, till we're sure this Specialist is off your tail."

"Oh, he'll be off all right. I'm hiring a specialist of my own. Tony 'The Chill.' "

"Tony Frabrizzio? Christ, boss, you're getting yourself in deep."

"Don't be such a pussy. Fabrizzio's the best hit man in the business. He's already accepted the contract. He'll be out here in twenty-four hours. And while I'm out of town, safe and sound, he'll hit this Specialist for me. We'll send a legend to kill a legend. The greatest hit man versus the so-called greatest mercenary. And I'm putting my money on Fabrizzio. Because Tony the Chill, he don't play fair."

Crackwell nodded. "That's the key to winning, all right."

Sullivan was angry and frustrated. First Bonnie tied his hands, warning him against hitting Legion directly, then Legion's connections had tied the court's hands. But it seemed that Legion wasn't the kind of guy to give up easily. He was going to try again, and that was going to be his last mistake. And Jack Sullivan was going to stick around and wait for that mistake.

He was at a health club, working out on the Nautilus machine, lying on his back and pressing three hundred pounds at the ceiling, working off his anger, sweating it out. Sullivan pumped iron until his muscles were twitching with exhaustion and he was slick with sweat. He got up, stretched, and went to the showers on legs that felt a little rubbery. He showered and went to the pool, swam thirty laps, all the time thinking, thinking . . .

But he came up with nothing. Nothing that would get Legion without endangering Bonnie and the tenants at Legion's building.

Heroin, he thought. Legion was quite probably a heroin smuggler.

Sullivan hated pushers. He'd seen heroin destroy a lot of good men in Vietnam. And it was eating up the United States of America from the inside, doing the USSR's work for it. Heroin and cocaine, draining billions of dollars into the pockets of foreign scumbags, money that should go back into America's economy. Burning out brains and livers and breaking hearts.

The more he thought about it, the angrier it made him. And the more determined he became to make sure Legion died. The heroin smuggling must be the key. Sullivan snorted at the thought of the government's "covert" watch on Legion. He knew it wasn't enough, that it probably wouldn't work. Legion would worm his way out of it. Still, Sullivan didn't want to wreck the government's investigation. He would just have to find a way to do his own investigation, without blowing theirs.

He climbed out of the pool, pleasantly tired but burning with renewed determination.

Tony "The Chill" Fabrizzio didn't look the part. He was a tall, sinewy, dapper man, a careful dresser. His face, too, was carefully dressed in a friendly or at least mild expression. His hair was prematurely silver, very contemporary in its cut. He wore cheerful suits, usually canary yellow or powder blue. He wore no gold chains, no dark glasses. There was nothing particularly sinister about him.

Just now, Fabrizzio was wearing a jogging suit. There

was an indoor track above the pool at the health club. He'd jogged around and around the track, now and then looking over the railing to check on Jack Sullivan. Fabrizzio was in pretty good shape, but he got tired running before Sullivan got tired swimming.

He stood at the rail, breathing hard, watching as Sullivan got out of the pool and crossed the wet blue tile to the locker room. He was an impressive sight, in the pool and out of it. Even from twenty-five yards away, Fabrizzio could see the bullet scars, white star shapes on Sullivan's arms, chest, back. . . . How could a man be wounded so many times and still live?

Yes, Sullivan was an impressive man. That made the game all the more interesting.

Fabrizzio hurried down the stairs and went into the locker room. He was careful to shower and change clothes in a section of the locker room where Sullivan wouldn't notice him. He changed hurriedly, left the gym, and just managed to catch sight of Sullivan turning the corner to the right. It was early evening. The rain had stopped; the gutters gurgled with the downpour that had ceased only a minute before. Passing cars were still running their windshield wipers. A pleasant scent of rain mixed with the minerals of the concrete. Fabrizzio felt good. He enjoyed the walk, and enjoyed the sense of stalking—of stalking without seeming to. And Fabrizzio was good at that.

Ahead, Sullivan stopped to look in the window of a sporting-goods store, admiring a display of fiberglass hunting bows. Fabrizzio wondered if Sullivan planned to use one of those bows on Legion.

Fabrizzio knew better than to stop when Sullivan stopped. Any unnatural movement in the flow of the pedestrian traffic would alert Sullivan's professional instincts. Fabrizzio kept walking, passing Sullivan, not even glancing at him, looking utterly relaxed and casual. He didn't look back to see where Sullivan was going. Fabrizzio might lose him this way, but if he did, it didn't matter at this stage of the game. He had perfected his kill technique over the years, and he was a great believer in studying the subject before setting up the hit. His research sometimes took a week or two. Sure, if the opportunity came up to hit the target without risking himself, and without leaving traces that would lead back to him, Fabrizzio would take that opportunity. There was a .45 Beretta in his autumn-gold suitjacket, patiently waiting its turn.

But usually, the ideal hit came after plenty of observation and planning. Fabrizzio didn't do things sloppily because sloppiness left a trail, like the crumbs on the table of a man who eats messily, and the cops could follow a trail of crumbs, right to the crumb who dropped them.

So Fabrizzio kept walking. He paused at the corner, looked both ways, then at the street sign, as if trying to decide which way to go. As if he was just a little bit lost. He stopped a cop walking by—yes, a cop—and asked directions to Times Square. That gave him an opportunity to turn sideways when he was talking to the cop, and he could see Jack Sullivan approaching. Fabrizzio watched with his peripheral vision, all the time seeming to look directly at the cop, who was patiently explaining how to find Forty-second Street to this rather pleasant-looking but evidently dense man in the autumn-gold suit. . . .

Preoccupied with his thoughts, Sullivan walked by. Going, fortunately, toward Times Square.

Fabrizzio followed. What will Sullivan do now? Fabrizzio wondered as they entered the region of porn theaters and head shops and whores and pushers selling phony drugs around Times Square. Will he buy a woman?

But Sullivan walked past several fairly attractive young whores, not so much as glancing at them when they asked, "Goin' out, honey? Wanna date?"

Sullivan kept walking, ignoring lurid movie marquees offering titles like *Do What You Want with Me* and *Pink Steel* and *Wet and Silky*.

But now, Fabrizzio saw, Sullivan was angling left, heading toward a door hawking "LIVE NUDE SEX." Fabrizzio was surprised. Sullivan didn't seem like the kind of man who would indulge himself that way. But perhaps he wasn't—perhaps he had business there.

Sullivan did have business at the sex show. He'd spotted an old acquaintance at the door, his personal informer, his pet snitch, Harry "Backdoor Man" Antonias. The surname was fake. He was a Cuban, and a part-time rock musician, and a full-time scam artist. Antonias wore a suit off the antique-clothing racks. He had black hair coiffed like early Elvis, and mirror sunglasses reflecting neon.

Antonias was looking the other way at a group of Japanese tourists when Sullivan approached. He was a barker for the Keyhole, paid $3.75 an hour to try to lure people off the street into the sex show.

"Gentlemen!" Antonias yelled. "I know you've got a fine eye for a fine piece of womanflesh. Slanted your eyes may be, but, my man, I know you see straight when you see these babes. They're pink and tender and pretty and hot to trot and they get off on it when they know somebody's watching the action and I do mean action 'cause you'll see it all in here and I mean *all* of it, right before your eyes. Hey, where you goin', my little yellow friends, come on-n-n, check it out, whatsa matter, you can't afford it? You didn't sell enough TV sets? Well, fuck you—hey!" The *hey!* came when an enormous bouncer from inside the club came up behind Antonias and sent him staggering with a thump on the back.

"Yuh dumbshit!" the bouncer croaked. He was an enormous, cretinous guy in a muscle shirt, with a crewcut topping his bullet head. His features were blurred from having been repeatedly punched; he was an ex-prizefighter. His brain had blurred from that, too.

"What's the big idea a shoving on me like that, Cueball!" Antonias protested, regaining his footing.

" 'Cause da boss he sent me to see whatcher doin' and I hear youse insultin' customas!"

"They weren't customers, that's why I was insulting them!"

"You don't tell people 'fuck youse' out here. Youse gotta tell em, come on in and see the pussy an' all like dat, you got it?"

"Listen, man, I don't need this shit. You're looking at a man with talent! An artist!"

"What you saying, that yer better'n me?" Cueball snarled, one of his ape arms grabbing for Antonias' neck.

But another arm came into the fray—Sullivan's, as he stepped up from the side and clamped a hand on Cueball's wrist. And squeezed. "Back off," he said, pushing Cueball back a step, and letting go.

"Who da fuck is dis asshole?" Cueball bellowed. "Ged outta here or I'll feed you to da gutter rats!"

Sullivan turned to Antonias. "You're quitting this job. I've got something new for you. Pay's better."

Antonias stared at him. "Uhh . . . is it going to get me killed?"

"Probably not."

"Probably? What you mean, *probably*?"

"Don't worry about it. Let's go—I'll buy you a drink and we'll talk."

"Now, wait a fuckin' minute here, pal. Dis here guy works for da Keyhole and I ain't letting some lunkhead off da street just—"

Sullivan said, "Let's go, Backdoor."

Cueball made a growling sound deep in his throat and charged at Sullivan's chest, his big hands up to close on his neck.

Sullivan seemed not to notice. He let Cueball get within six inches of grabbing him.

Then he ducked, sidestepped, and whirled, coming around behind Cueball and kicking him in the pants to send him head first into a heap of bulging garbage bags.

Bottles and cups and condoms went flying. Cueball roared and got to his feet. He turned and threw a bag of bottles at Sullivan's head. Sullivan ducked that too. It went over his head and smashed into a pimp, knocking his enormous white hat off his head.

A crowd began to gather around them; the street dealers and pickpockets and every manner of sidewalk scum gathered in a circle to hoot and laugh and shout encouragement to both men. Cueball raised his fists. Sullivan smiled and raised his, boxer-style. The men circled one another, dancing like heavyweights.

"I'm gonna kick your ass!" Cueball shouted. "I was a pro!"

Antonias groaned and hissed, "Cueball, don't do it. You don't know who this guy *is*!"

Cueball drove a right at Sullivan's gut as Sullivan danced to the side. The blow landed on the window of a parked car and the glass webbed around the impact hole.

Cueball jerked his fist loose and rushed at Sullivan, swinging wildly, slathering with fury.

Sullivan dodged each blow easily and landed four of his own in rapidfire, less than a second and a half for all four blows—two to Cueball's ribs, one to his neck, one to his chin. Sullivan had gotten a good look at Cueball's face and felt a little sorry for the guy: he didn't want to mess up his nose any more than it already was.

Cueball staggered, but kept coming, seeming to get some of his old training reflexes back. He landed one on Sullivan's rock-hard stomach muscles. Sullivan responded with three more, driving the man steadily back toward the door of the Keyhole. Cueball was big but out of shape and he was already becoming winded. His movements were heavier and heavier, as if gravity were increasing around him.

Sullivan tired of the game. He didn't like the hooting crowd around him. He wasn't into humiliating anyone. And the cops might show up any second. One of them might recognize him. He had to end it.

He blocked a right from Cueball, and looked past him at the stairway. The stairs into the showplace went down. It was in the basement of the building. Sullivan sent two quick flurries of punches to Cueball's head, forcing him back toward the stairs, throwing him off balance. Cueball lurched into the doorway, and Sullivan kicked him hard in the middle of the chest—a karate kick—but not so hard it would break anything.

"Check out the girls for me, Cueball!" Sullivan said, as the bouncer went over backward and slid down the stairs, bouncing on his ass to lie stunned at the bottom.

The crowd cheered. Sullivan ignored them. He and Antonias left, fast.

A few of the street cruds tried to tag along, telling Sullivan what a great guy he was and since he was a great guy they'd give him a deal on some fine drugs, anything you want, we got it pal . . . Sullivan gave them a look, and the look was enough. They melted away.

Sullivan and Antonias went into the cocktail lounge tucked away in a corner of a Howard Johnson's. Sullivan ordered Irish whiskey, Antonias ordered a double screwdriver.

Antonias had to suck down half his drink before he worked up the nerve to ask, "So, Sullivan, my main man, uh—what's this job that's *probably* not going to get me killed."

Sullivan glanced around. They were alone at the bar. At the far end, the bartender watched a football game on the wall-mounted color TV.

Sullivan said, "What do you know about a guy named Legion? Landlord, maybe a drug smuggler."

"Not a damn thing and that's the truth."

"How about a guy named Crackwell? That ring a bell?"

"Nope."

"Take off those goddamn dark glasses." Antonias took off the glasses. Sullivan looked at his eyes. "You know nothing about Crackwell or Legion?" he asked. Antonias shook his head. Sullivan could see he was telling the truth. "Okay. Then you'd better get your ass in gear and find out." He took two fifty-dollar bills from his brown leather flight jacket and passed them to Antonias. Out of habit, Antonias palmed them so no one would see the exchange, though there was nothing illegal in it.

"Okay. Any idea where I start asking, Kimosabe?"

"Try Spanish Harlem first. A Hundred-tenth Street. Maybe pretend you want to work for the guy. You heard he was hiring strong-arms."

"You got it. How I reach you?"

Sullivan gave him a phone number. "More money coming if you find something good for me. I know where the guy lives—but he doesn't piss in his own yard. I need to know where he's doing his dealing, who the intermediaries are, what their system is, anything you can find out."

"I'll get right on it." Antonias started to get up.

Sullivan pulled him back onto the stool. "I know where to find you, man. So don't be running off with my coin and getting loaded. It's going to be a big temptation, with all that dope up there. Don't do it. Buy a little reefer or something if you have to, to be one of the boys. But don't fuck with the heavy drugs."

"Your solicitude is touching."

"I just want to make sure you don't nod out when you're supposed to be working."

"I got all that stuff under control, man. My vices are girls and booze now. With, as you say, the occasional reefer."

"Make it very occasional. Now, head up there."

"Later."

Antonias sucked his drink down in one gulp, and left. Sullivan took his time finishing his whiskey.

In another part of the restaurant, Fabrizzio drank a coffee and pretended to eat some greasy french fries. But all the time, he watched Sullivan, without ever seeming to.

He regretted not knowing what it was Sullivan had paid the young rocker to do. But he would find out. He'd learn all about the Specialist.

And then he'd kill him.

8

Caught in the Cross Hairs

Across the street from the old brownstone where Sullivan was staying was a ratty hotel, the Belle Starr. Fabrizzio took up residence at the Belle Starr, with some regret.

It had been a shabby hotel from its start in the forties. Its decor was styled around a western theme, with cobwebbed deer antlers over the front desk and badly executed murals of cowboys and Indians in the hallway. The lobby's walls were crudely painted to resemble logs in a log cabin. It had been bought by Pakistanis, like many cheap Manhattan hotels. About half the rooms were used by whores from nearby Eighty-sixth Street. They didn't hawk their wares on the hotel's street, but once they found a buyer they brought him here, where he paid ten dollars to use the room for a half-hour. A half-hour was usually about fifteen minutes longer than the john really needed.

Fabrizzio had a front room, overlooking the street, where he could keep an eye on Sullivan's building. He was not happy with his accommodations, but he could easily adapt to his surroundings. He'd changed his style of dress, making it shabby enough to fit the hotel. He didn't want to be conspicuous, not to anyone.

Fabrizzio had been watching Sullivan for three days. The first day, he followed when Sullivan went out jogging, running behind at a discreet distance. Sullivan had jogged to Central Park, and then had circled the reservoir twice. On the second day, Fabrizzio had posted himself behind a statue near the path Sullivan used to get to the reservoir. He posted himself thirty minutes before Sullivan went out for his morning run. Sullivan came by, like clockwork, at seven A.M. There weren't many joggers around so early. That would make this a reasonable spot for the hit, Fabrizzio reasoned. Pretty good cover, good withdrawal route through the screen of trees around the statue. But best to check further, see if an even more convenient killing ground offered itself from Sullivan's daily routine.

But apart from his morning run, Sullivan did nothing else predictably. He spent most of his time in the building. Much of it in the apartment with the woman. They would spend hours at a time in there with the shades drawn. Was he really making love to her for so long? What else would they be doing? They had no television and it was inconceivable, from what Fabrizzio was able to find out about Sullivan, that they would be taking drugs. So they were making love all that time, and once more Fabrizzio was impressed.

Sullivan never went out with the woman. She went out alone, or he left alone, but always one of them stayed, probably to watch over the building.

Sullivan's apartment faced the street, the southeast corner. But it didn't matter—the shades were always pulled at Sullivan's.

Sometimes Fabrizzio saw him check the roof. The big man would wander the rooftops of his apartment building and the two adjacent like some restless panther. Now and then he would bend to check on something Fabrizzio couldn't make out. Booby traps? No, someone innocent might be hurt by booby traps on the roof, and Sullivan's pattern was that of a man always watching out for the innocents. But Sullivan might have set some kind of warning system up on the roof, to tell him if anyone had moved about on it recently.

There was no pattern to Sullivan's visits to the roof. He seemed to be deliberately timing the inspections randomly. If Fabrizzio were to shoot the Specialist when he was on the rooftop—perhaps using a rifle and sniper-scope from the Belle Starr rooftop—he would have to watch until he saw Sullivan up there, run up to his own roof, set up the rifle, and fire while the big man was still on the adjacent roof. Possible but not tidy. Fabrizzio liked things orderly.

There was an alternative. Wait until Sullivan came back from jogging. Be waiting for him in the stairway. Sullivan took a small gun with him when he went jogging. He had it clipped to the back of his belt, under his sweatshirt. Fabrizzio had seen the bulge of it. But if Fabrizzio were quick enough, waiting and ready, Sulli-van would have no chance to use it. Only . . .

Only Fabrizzio realized he didn't want to get that close to Sullivan, unless it were absolutely necessary. The man's reputation was legendary. Who knew how good his reflexes were? There was even a sense of . . . of some extraordinary intuitive awareness around the man. Fabrizzio was simply afraid to get near him.

Afraid? Was he, Tony the Chill, afraid of a target? Ridiculous.

But. Extra precaution must be taken with this man Sullivan.

Yes, the best killing ground would seem to be the park.

Fabrizzio set the briefcase up on a tree stump in the cluster of elms ten yards behind the statue. He glanced around. A morning fog wreathed the gray-black trunks of trees; clumps of shrubbery bristled, squat between the trees. No one in sight. He opened the briefcase. Inside, unassembled, was a custom-made 30.06 hunt-ing rifle with a folding stock and a telescopic sight. A lot of professionals would be surprised if they knew that Tony the Chill used so light a gun. But he found that it worked best for him. It would punch a nice big hole in a man. No question about that.

Fabrizzio looked at his watch. Six-forty-five. If the Specialist were running true to form, he would arrive in fifteen minutes. Flexing his hands for warmth, humming a Mozart cantata under his breath, Fabrizzio drew a pair of ultrathin black leather gloves over his hands, tugging them taut on his fingers. Then he assembled the gun, screwing the barrel onto the breach, unfolding the stock, clicking the scope into place, sighting experimentally down the scope, adjusting it, sighting again. He dry-fired it a few times, the faint snick of the hammer falling on the empty chamber like the sound of a mouse's neck crunched in the jaws of a cat.

He sighted through the scope at the head of the statue, a fifty-year-old bronze of some early New York mogul. The head of the bronze looked strangely outsize in the scope; even the leaves of the tree beyond it seemed unnaturally defined and important.

He lowered the rifle and glanced at his watch. Seven minutes. He loaded the rifle. He laid the briefcase aside and knelt beside the stump. He set his elbows on the stump, the gun propped in his hands, stock snugged against his shoulder. Sullivan would soon jog along the trail up the hill in front of the statue. Fabrizzio would see him jog up the slope from the left. Sullivan would pass in front of the statue. He would emerge on the right side, directly in front of Fabrizzio's gun, about thirty-two yards away. Fabrizzio would shoot Sullivan through the side of the head.

Fabrizzio glanced at his watch. About three minutes. He chambered a round.

Movement to the left. Sullivan, jogging up the trail, seen in flickers through the intermittent screen of bushes and trees.

Fabrizzio looked through the scope. His thumb flicked the safety off the rifle. His finger rested on the trigger. Sullivan jogged to the statue. Fabrizzio took a deep breath. As Fabrizzio let the breath out, Sullivan passed behind the statue. Before taking another breath, while his body was still, Fabrizzio planned to sight in on Sullivan as Sullivan emerged from behind the statue and track to follow him. Then he would pull the trigger.

But Sullivan didn't come out from behind the statue. Fabrizzio waited. Two seconds, three, four. Nothing.

Fabrizzio raised his head, remembered to breathe, then stood, lowering the rifle. Something was wrong. The hair rose on the back of his neck. He felt a chill which seemed to course through him maliciously, mocking him.

Where was Sullivan?

Fabrizzio felt a tickle of warmth on his cheek. He glanced left, east. The sun! The morning sun had risen enough to slant a few rays into the trees—Sullivan must have seen the light glancing off the rifle barrel!

Fabrizzio's mouth went dry. He backed away from the statue and turned to slip into the brush. He paused, crouching behind a thick green bush, listening. He heard a crunch of footsteps in autumn leaves. He raised his head a little to peer through the space between the leaves at the top of the bush.

He saw a big human silhouette in a bank of fog. The Specialist!

Fabrizzio raised the rifle, pressed it through the leaves, and fired, twice. But his nerves were shaken—he was used to being the stalker, not the stalked. And the fog was thick over there. He missed.

He cursed and turned to run through the brush.

The Beretta Brigadier in his hand, Sullivan loped up the hillside, peering through the mist. It seemed to make ghostly shapes out of every bush and tree trunk. Whoever it was might be waiting for him along the way—or he might have run.

Something else glimmered on the ground ahead of him, beside a big green bush. He bent and picked up two empty rifle shells. Thirty-aught-six. The two shots that had missed him. He scanned the brush nearby, half-expecting to be shot at again any moment. But all was silence, excpt for bird twitterings and the rustling of squirrels in the branches.

Sullivan had a feeling his attacker had split. He was a long-range shooter, maybe a professional—at least, he'd evidently known Sullivan's running route, which meant he'd been watching him, setting him up. And using a hunting rifle.

Yeah. A pro. But a pro who'd made a big mistake.

He'd underestimated the Specialist's awareness level. Sullivan had learned the trick in Nam. You had to be constantly alert, aware, and yet not drive yourself mad with looking. You had to keep scanning, even when things were at their most peaceful—and yet not become paranoid. Paranoia made for inefficiency. So you learned to take comfort in all the order and peacefulness you saw when you scanned for enemies. But you didn't let it lull you. You kept scanning, until it finally became a habit.

Scanning the brush as he ran up the trail, Sullivan had seen the telltale flash of light reflecting off the rifle barrel through the screen of brush. He hadn't seen the shooter, though. By the time he'd backed up, keeping the statue between himself and the gunman, and circled around, coming up from down the hill, the guy had taken to the brush.

Sullivan turned and trotted through the small woods, back to the stone fence by the sidewalk. Jogging would have to be in a different neighborhood from now on. A different one every day.

Frustrated, Fabrizzio paced his shabby room, smoking a Balkan Sobranie, glancing now and then at the window. Had the man seen him? He thought not. Still, if he had, he would come hunting for him. And it was said he had killed hundreds of men.

There must not be more delay. He, Fabrizzio, must kill this Sullivan, and quickly. If possible, he must do it tonight.

9

Which the Hunter and Which the Hunted?

Sullivan paused on the corner of 110th Street and Third Avenue. He lit a Lucky Strike, cupping his hand against the wind. He blew smoke into the air, watching the damp breeze swirl it away. He glanced at his watch. It was ten P.M. The night was cold. He could see his breath, and he cadged warmth from the cigarette in his hand.

The cold had driven the street activity into the Hispanic Social clubs, into the bars and tenement apartments, into free-basing parlors and dope-shooting galleries. To the west was a row of tenements, most of them burnt out and deserted except for a few squatters. To the east was a red brick canyon of housing-project high-rises; the grassy areas between the buildings were flecked with trash, wax cups, cigarette wrappers and newspapers that rolled soggily in the wind.

Antonias came across the street from uptown, wearing a black pea coat and a black-watch ap. "Whus happenin', my main man?" he said.

"All Spanish guys talk like black street people when they're talking English?" Sullivan asked.

"Yo man, that's musician talk." Antonias grinned. "You're looking at Mr. Funky. In person."

"Okay, Funky. Let's get some coffee."

They went south half a block to a Spanish-Chinese restaurant. "The story with these places," Antonias said as they settled down with coffee and a plate of fried plantains, in a warm booth near the back, "is there was a colony of Chinese in Havana and when the revolution broke out they left Cuba but they picked up this Cuban cuisine, see, so a bunch of them started Chinese and Cuban restaurants in—"

"That all you've found out for my hundred bucks?"

"Oh, a little bit more." He looked around to see if they were alone, an unnecessary act since the place was empty except for them and the yawning waitress at the counter.

"Okay, this's what I found out." He sipped his coffee, then said, "There's a contract out on you."

"That I figured out. Somebody took a couple shots at me. You find out who it is?"

Munching plantains, Antonias said, "I heard it was some *el supremo* gun wizard from Chicago. I don't know who. But I heard it was Crackwell hired him. That's pretty much all I got—got it from a friend of mine worked in that numbers joint you busted up. Oh, except for one thing. I got a name. Carlos Ajidas. Some kind of gofer for Crackwell. Shows up at a club around here. A free-basing parlor, you know? He brings in the dope and the coke, picks up the money. Mean little guy. A *pistolero*, they said."

"You know where this parlor is?"

"I know which building, but not where in the building."

"Close enough. I'll find my way."

"Fourth building west from the corner you were standing on," Antonias told him.

"You think Ajidas is there now?"

"Way I heard it, he shows up about nine-thirty, hangs out for a while, maybe an hour, goes to another stop . . ."

"Then he just might be there." Sullivan stood and

tossed two fifties on the table. "Take the coffee and the plantains out of that. And keep up the good work."

"Okay, man. Watch your ass—the place is guarded."

Tying the belt of his leather trench coat, Sullivan walked out into the bitter wind.

He walked to the corner, turned left, and strolled four buildings down, to the building Antonias had indicated. It was completely boarded over and dead-looking. The front door was gaping wide, but Sullivan thought he saw movement on the roof, just a black shape moving against the dark gray of the overcast sky.

Sullivan decided to plunge headlong into this one.

He walked up the old granite stoop and stepped inside. It was dark but a little light spilled into the front hall from the streetlamp on the corner. Another faint light spilled down from the second floor, outlining the top steps of the first flight in lines of shadow. Sullivan took the gun from his shoulder holster and held it down at his side. He was carrying the Beretta tonight.

He started up the steps. They creaked under his boots. He stopped at the turn to the second flight. Someone was on the flight above him. "Who the fuck is that?" he said. The stranger was shrouded in shadow. So was Sullivan's gun.

Sullivan said, "I'm here to see Ajidas." He started once more up the steps. The man above him took a step back.

"Hold it right there."

"Ajidas is expecting me." And Sullivan kept coming, not too slow and not too fast.

He heard the click of a hammer being pulled back on a gun. He saw a faint gleam about waist-high along the length of a pistol barrel. The uneven light from above picked out a corner of the man's face. One fear-widened eye, and a sweat-beaded black forehead. So this wasn't Ajidas.

"I said hold it there, man. I'll burn you."

Sullivan said, "Take it easy. I'm not a cop. You want to get in trouble with Ajidas? I'm from Crackwell, man.

You a spotter out here?" Sullivan was on the top step, talking like a man trying to soothe a testy bull. "Easy there, now, easy . . ."

The guy lowered his gun. "Take me to him," Sullivan said.

Sullivan's eyes were beginning to adjust to the dark. He made out a tall black guy with a heavy mustache and a hard-planed, sweat-coated face. The kind of sweat-coating a man gets in reaction to a hit of heroin. A recent hit. "They got some good stuff tonight?" Sullivan asked.

"The shit's good, man," the guard said, turning to lead the way up the stairs.

They went up two flights. The light increased. It was coming from a window in a door. Someone had cut out most of the upper half of the door and replaced it with thick bullet-proofed window glass. There was a scoop-shaped hole cut in the glass through which money could be passed for admission. It looked like the cashier's window of a movie theater. Except the guy on the other side wore a gun in a shoulder holster.

He was a Spanish guy wearing a yellow baseball cap; a stub of a cigar was clenched in his teeth. He squinted past the cigar smoke at Sulivan, scowling. "Who zat guy?" he asked the guard. "Hey, what the hell you doin', man—"

"Says he's got an appointment with Ajidas," the guard grunted as he unlocked the door.

"Well, damn, don't unlock the fuckin' door till we check it with Ajidas!"

But it was too late. The stoned guard had turned the key in the lock. He realized his mistake—would have taken the key out, left the door locked—only Sullivan didn't give him the chance.

The Specialist gave his best imitation of a guard on the Rams' defensive line. He plowed a shoulder into the guy, ramming him into the door, knocking the door open. It swung inward. The black guy fell on his face. The Hispanic tugged the gun loose, a .38, training it on

Sullivan. But Sullivan snapped the Beretta up and squeezed off a single shot, the round punching a neat round hole in the Hispanic's forehead. The .38 tumbled from limp fingers.

Sullivan kept moving, plunging into the room, the Beretta in both hands, tracking left and right, looking for another assailant. No one with a gun. Shocked faces looked up at him from mattresses lined along the floor. Eight people, all colors. Five of them had small glass pipes, and used butane hand torches to melt ether-treated cocaine into free-basing chunks, sucking down the smoke of the purified drug for quick rushes of pleasure. After each rush of pleasure there was a down, a crash, a trough of depression, and then all the free-baser could think of was getting back *up* again. Only, the more they did the drug, the deeper the *depressions* were and the less the highs felt really up, till at last they were locked into a desperate search for a repeat of the initial rush, a repeat that never quite came.

Automatons, Sullivan thought with disgust. Pathetic pleasure robots. Pavlov's dogs.

Some of them looked at him, a man with a gun in his hand who'd shot a man in front of them moments before, and kept right on sucking at their pipes, their eyes glazed with the masturbatory search for the distracting neurological jolt.

Others backed away, panicked, whining like terrified animals.

Sullivan noticed a door at the far end of the room. He started toward it. Then he heard a sound behind him. He felt a tingling in the middle of his back, at the spot where he knew he was about to be shot.

He leapt to the left, throwing himself down, rolling, coming up facing the door, Beretta in hand.

The black guard was there, firing the .38 at the spot where Sullivan had been before. His heroin-blurred senses reacted slowly and the round missed Sullivan but buried itself in the chest of a haggard, hollow-eyed man against the far wall. The free-basing pipe fell from the man's hands and smashed on the floor. The cocaine spilled from the pipe. One of the other men scrabbled to claw at the fallen drug, eager to scavenge it from a corpse.

Sullivan and the guard aimed their guns at one another. But Sullivan's reflexes were not dulled by drugs. He fired first, sending two rounds through the left corner of the guard's forehead; the rounds emerged from the right-rear corner of the man's head, taking two-thirds of his brain along with them and sending it splattering against the wall. He fell stone dead as the door opened at the other end of the room. A figure emerged. He was a smallish man with a goatee and eyes like black beetles crouched in his skull. He swore in Spanish and pointed a .45 automatic at Sullivan. He fired twice but without carefully aiming; both shots whistled over Sullivan's right shoulder.

Sullivan had a feeling he'd found his man. "Ajidas!" he shouted. "Hold it!"

But the other man turned and ran back into the room he'd come out of.

Sullivan ran down the length of the barren room, under the flyspecked naked bulb dangling overhead, across bare boards, past a man vomiting in a corner, past another man shooting up a second load of heroin and shaking his head slowly at his hallucinations, past a woman giving head to a man doing free-base— both of them had been doing this during the gunplay, oblivious . . .

To the door.

Sullivan kicked the door in, then flattened to one side of it. He waited three beats. No one fired at the door. He heard a clattering sound. The son of a bitch was going down the fire escape.

Sullivan stepped into the room and looked around. There was a table at one end, with a little white powder and scales still on it, a bare lightbulb burning overhead, and except for the open window letting in a blast of cold air that scattered the white powder, that was all.

Sullivan swore and moved to the window, snaked out

onto the fire escape. He climbed down, hands cold on the icy metal, pausing once to look over the rail. There were two of them, two stories below. A blond guy, and Ajidas following.

Sullivan clattered down after them, wincing as a blast of cold air swept a handful of icy rain in his face. Another gust came—but this time it brought snow with it. Sullivan glanced up, surprised. A glittering swirl of snowflakes tumbled from the sky.

Down below, Ajidas was just dropping to the ground from the last rung of the fire-escape ladder. Sullivan had narrowed the gap, but he was still on the second-floor fire escape. He went to the corner of the fire-escape landing and knelt; he laid his gun arm across the rail, clasped the gun between both hands, and aimed very carefully. Ajidas was about thirty feet from the bottom of the fire escape, running east, toward Third Avenue. The blond had run in the opposite direction. Sullivan trained the gun on Ajidas' right-rear thigh. Ajidas was forty feet away now. Forty-five, fifty . . .

Sullivan squinted through the snowflakes settling on his eyelashes, clinging to the barrel of the gun.

Ajidas was now sixty feet away. The snow thickened, obscuring the running figure. Sullivan fired twice.

Ajidas screamed and fell on his face in the middle of the deserted street.

Sullivan put the Beretta in his pocket, ran down the stairs, dropped to the sidewalk. He ran after Ajidas. The drug runner was up, stumbling onward. But he wouldn't go far with two holes in his leg.

Sullivan drew the Beretta.

Ajidas heard the sound of Sullivan's bootsteps behind him. He turned and fired another ragged salvo with the .45. But he was a bad shot, and he was rattled.

Sullivan kept coming. Ajidas wailed and turned, falling on his face. The snow swirled down around him.

Sullivan ran up to him, reached down, jerked the man to his feet by his collar, shook him once hard.

Ajidas dropped the gun. Sullivan kicked it into a gutter; it fell through a sewer grate into the rushing water.

The Specialist dragged the drug runner to a nearby doorway. It was a dark doorway. Ajidas hissed, "Come on, man, whatchoo doin'? I didn't do nothin' to you! We got a deal already! The bagman already came today!"

Ajidas thought he was a cop, Sullivan realized. "Yeah? I didn't hear about it. Maybe I let you go if you tell me: who's the bagman take the money to?"

"Krinsky, man, Detective Krinsky!"

"Uh-huh. Well, I got a surprise for you, I ain't a cop so you can't pay me off with what you pay them. I don't take bribes. What I want from you is facts."

"I don't know nothin'! Lemme go before I bleed to death, man!"

Sullivan spun Ajidas around and slammed him up against the concrete wall, banging the back of his head. Ajidas gritted his teeth and clenched his eyes shut with pain. Sullivan slapped him, twice, backhanded. Blood ran from Ajidas' nose.

"My leg!" Ajidas groaned. "My leg!"

"Give!" Sullivan snarled. "How is Crackwell smuggling the stuff in!"

"I don't know—" Sullivan slammed him against the wall again. And this time, Sullivan brought the barrel of the Beretta up, shoving its muzzle tip into Ajidas' nose. Ajidas opened his eyes and stared in horror down the length of the barrel. Sullivan dug it more deeply into Ajidas' nostril. "Sounds to me like you got a sinus condition," Sullivan said. "You want me to clear that up for you?"

"No, man, don't do it!"

"Then stop bullshitting me!"

"Easyair, man! Brings it in on Easyair, he owns the company through some kind of lawyer so nobody can trace it to him, you know? They bring the stuff in furniture from Thailand. Hollow legs. They route it through Sicily. That's all I know!"

"What about this end? Where do they take it after they get it out of the furniture?"

"A house out in Hoboken. The stuff comes in at Newark and they take it to Hoboken. I never been out there, I don't know where exactly, I swear!"

Ajidas made a sudden movement and Sullivan felt an icy stinging at his left hip. He looked down and saw that Ajidas had stuck a knife in him. He'd been trying to stick it up into his kidneys but hadn't been able to reach that far in the awkward angle. Ajidas pulled the knife free and tried again. Sullivan stepped back—the knife slashed by his stomach, caught in the leather of his coat.

Sullivan shrugged and pulled the trigger of the Beretta.

Ajidas had no more sinus trouble after that.

Why? Fabrizzio asked himself. Why had he missed when he'd shot at Sullivan in the park? The fog? The fog was just an excuse. He'd seen the man's silhouette, he should have been able to hit him.

Fear. The answer was fear. The guy rattled him somehow. The Specialist made him nervous. Sullivan seemed so alert, so self-contained, and he looked dangerous. As if shooting him might set off an explosion of some kind that would kill the shooter too.

So Fabrizzio was forcing himself to face up to Sullivan.

He waited now on the stairs between the second and third floor of Sullivan's building, a .357 Magnum in his hands. It was nearly midnight. A radio commercial yammered inanely from somewhere in the building; otherwise, it was quiet. The tenants had replaced the front door of the building and Fabrizzio had been forced to enter from the roof. Sooner or later, Sullivan would come up those stairs. He would walk into a trap.

So why was Fabrizzio feeling so fluttery inside? He had set the trap, not Sullivan. He was lying in wait, preparing to spring the trap, not Sullivan. The pistol in his hand was a big one. It would blow Sullivan's head off his shoulders. He, Fabrizzio, was the hunter, not Sullivan.

So why was he afraid? Why did the sound of the door opening three floors below make his hands shake?

I am a professional, he thought. I have killed a hundred and fifteen men.

The Specialist will die, like all the others.

10
The Duel Begins

Sullivan was brooding as he came into the building. The pain flashed in his hip when he walked. But the wound was slight; it didn't slow him down much. What bothered him more was how to hit Legion without involving Bonnie and the people in Moreland's building. But maybe that question was a red herring. Maybe if Legion disappeared the cops would simply assume one of his underworld connections had taken him out—nothing too surprising when a heroin smuggler got himself aced. The tenants were tangling with Legion in court, but that wouldn't amount to proof they had hired the Specialist to kill Legion.

Still, he had to make sure that no one connected the Specialist with this building. Best if the Specialist weren't brought into this thing at all—make it look as if Legion were killed by his competitors.

But the underworld knew that Legion had hired a hit man to kill the Specialist. And if the underworld knew, then so did Detective Krinsky. So it looked like the Specialist would be implicated.

Sullivan shrugged. He reached the second floor, turning toward the third.

On the third floor, Bonnie Roland stepped out of Sullivan's subletted apartment, on her way to see

Moreland. She paused at the stairs. Looking down the stairwell she saw a strange man in a black coat standing a few steps below. The man had silvery hair—and a gun in his hand which he was now pointing down the stairs at someone.

"Jack, look out!" Bonnie shouted.

She turned, opened her door, and ran back inside, scrabbling for her gun in the pocket of her coat hanging on the hook behind the door.

Two thunderous gunshots rang out from the hallway.

She grabbed the .25 and ran back out into the hall. A man ran past her, straight-arming her as he came, the flat of his palm striking her in the middle of the chest, knocking her over backward. He kept going up the stairs.

Sullivan smacked a fresh clip into the Beretta and ran up the stairs. His hip-wound burned; he felt fresh blood running hot and wet down his leg.

Bonnie was lying in the doorway of his apartment. He ran up to her, and she sat up. He helped her to her feet. "I'm okay," she said, cocking her pistol. "He's up there."

Sullivan ran ahead up the stairs, with Bonnie close on his heels.

Though each had gotten off a shot, neither Sullivan nor the assassin had scored. The assassin's .357 had rammed a fist-sized hole through the wall near Sullivan's head. Sullivan had been mounting the steps, and had paused at the turn. He wasn't sure why he had paused. Just . . . a feeling. A sense of danger. But he'd chosen to pause at the same instant that the would-be killer had chosen to shoot, throwing the guy's aim off. Sullivan had returned fire, knocking out a chunk of a wooden banister post, and the assassin had run for it.

Now Sullivan kicked open the door to the roof, and stood back. No one fired at the door. The glow from the hallway spilled out onto the snow, making the blanket of white sparkle with a long streak of bluish light. A

neat pattern of footsteps ran across the snow from the
door to the edge of the building.

Bonnie said, "If you go out there you'll be a sitting
duck. You'll be silhouetted against the light."

He nodded. "Anyway, I think he's gone. Lit out."

"What makes you so sure?"

"He's a long-range assassin. Shoots you when you're
not looking or not expecting it. He rings the doorbell,
you answer, he blows three holes in your chest. He
snipes from rooftops, plants bombs in cars. Shoots poi-
son darts. But he's not a firefight man."

"How do you know?"

"This is the second time he's tried for me. He's
showing his style."

"The second time! Why didn't you tell me!"

"I would've. Come on." He closed and locked the
roof door, and they went back down to his apartment.

They sat on the bed—well out of the line of fire from
the window. Sullivan was in his underwear, while she
put a dressing on his wound.

She hadn't said anything since he'd told her how he
got the wound. She finished, and he sat drinking a beer,
thinking.

"Jack—" she began.

"I know," he said.

"You know what?"

"You were going to tell me I shouldn't have gone out
and rousted Ajidas. I promised not to kill anyone on
this gig, and it's provoking Legion." He grinned at her.
"Right?"

"Yeah, more or less. So how about it?"

"What did you want me to do? Stand around and let
Legion's hit man pick me off? The game changes when
people start shooting at me with sniper scopes."

"I see what you mean."

"I have to take Legion out. That's the bottom line.
From what I can find out, he's a bulldog kind of guy.
When he's got his teeth locked onto someone's leg, he

doesn't let go till he tears a piece out of it. He's not going to give up. He's going to keep hiring guys, if this one fails, till one of them gets me. So I've got to do the only thing I can do to keep him from hiring them. Kill him."

"Is that really the only way?"

Sullivan shrugged. "The guy deserves it anyway. You know that and I know it. I can take him out, and the city can take over this building. I'll be careful to see no one here is implicated. And I'm going to try to do it in a way that doesn't blow the federal investigation of Legion's connections with his drug-dealing cronies."

She sighed. "Okay. But not from here. You've shown us how to defend the place. I doubt if he'll send anyone else around before he gets you out of the way."

Sullivan nodded. "Tomorrow I find a new base of operations. But tonight . . ."

He ran his hand down her cheek, down her breasts, down her waist to dip between her thighs, as he bent to kiss her neck.

"Jack! You're wounded!"

"I'm not wounded where it matters."

She kept up the pretense of resistance for a few minutes, but she didn't try very hard, and he knew she was only teasing. And in a few minutes she was begging him to tear her panties off with his teeth.

Afterward they were hot and sweaty, and Bonnie said, "Let's take a shower together."

"Sure," Sullivan said. "But you're getting a *cold* shower, you insatiable bitch."

Sullivan picked her up in his arms and carried her to the bathroom. She kicked her legs playfully, pretending to pound his chest with her fists.

He walked across the room with her in his arms, and their silhouette showed on the drapes for a moment.

Across the street on the roof, Fabrizzio aimed the grenade launcher and fired. The M79 round smashed through the window.

Sullivan was just stepping into the bathroom. The round struck the floor behind him. The bathroom wall protected Sullivan from the blast. But Bonnie, in his arms, was only halfway through the open door, her head and neck exposed. The shock wave knocked her from his arms. A thunderclap shook the room. Shrapnel whistled and smoke filled the apartment. Bonnie, on the floor, made a small soft noise, and lay still. A piece of shrapnel had struck her in the neck.

Dizzy, his ears ringing from the explosion, Sullivan ran to the next room, grabbed a blanket, and returned to the bathroom. He wrapped Bonnie in the blanket and picked her up in his arms. He carried her into the bedroom. A small fire had broken out in the charred remains of the bed. A four-foot-wide hole had been torn in the floor; both windows were blown out. Smoke choked the room. A portion of the ceiling was gone. A babble of voices came from above, below, and the hallway. Coughing from the smoke, he moved to the door. He reached out, supporting Bonnie on his forearm, and unlatched it, stepping into the hall.

Moreland, Eric, and Berrigan were there, gaping. "Call an ambulance!" Sullivan shouted.

Eric ran to his apartment to make the call. Moreland followed Sullivan down the stairs. Sullivan laid Bonnie out on the new tile of the downstairs hallway. Berrigan nudged Sullivan and handed him a bathrobe. Sullivan looked at him, puzzled. Why had the old man given him a bathrobe?

"You got no clothes, my boy," Berrigan whispered.

Sullivan looked down at himself. He was nude. "Oh, thanks," he said mechanically. He put the robe on, tying it at the waist.

"What—" Moreland began.

"Some asshole's been trying to kill me," Sullivan growled, taking Bonnie's pulse. It was there, but weak. "He just tried again. A grenade. We were in the bathroom. She was hit by flak."

Eric stood at the head of the stairs, shouting, "Ambulance is on its way!"

"There's a fire in my room," Sullivan told him.

"We put it out with a fire extinguisher!"

Sullivan nodded, and tore off a piece of the blanket to make a temporary pressure bandage. Bonnie had two wounds he could see, one in the base of the skull, another in the neck. The fragment had just missed her jugular vein.

Sullivan stood and looked down at her. Something wrenched inside him. It was as if a small animal had been living inside him, but had been asleep—and how it woke and found itself trapped in his chest, trying to claw its way out.

It was not a good feeling.

Lily, and then Beth. The two women he'd loved, both killed because they'd been close to him.

Not again, he thought. *Not again.*

He was a strong man, was Jack Sullivan. But he was a man. And he was afraid he could not bear it if Bonnie died too—because of him.

If she died, he just might go mad.

A siren howled nearer and nearer, out in the street; the police and fire departments arriving. The sirens grew and blended into one wall, and it was as if it screamed the rage and hurt he felt. It screamed for him. It rose to ear-splitting intensity as the vehicles turned onto his street, and it echoed loudly within him. He turned and slammed a fist into the wall. His fist was buried in the plaster; he was up to his wrist in the wall. He pulled it out, and pieces of plaster fell. His knuckles bled through the white powder caking them.

The ambulance attendants came in and began to lift Bonnie onto a stretcher.

Moreland moved close to whisper to Sullivan. "You've got to get out of here—cops coming up the steps. I'll make up a story. I'll say she was staying there alone, it was a reprisal against her from the landlord for her investigation. It's half-true—he probably wanted her dead, too. I won't mention you. They'll investigate Legion for this—they have to."

"There won't be any point," Sullivan said, his voice flat, icy. "By the time they get around to investigating him, he'll be dead."

He went upstairs to borrow some clothing from Eric. On the way, he stopped off at his apartment to get his jacket, his gun, and his ammunition, all of it undamaged in the explosion because it had been locked in the closet. He was going to need the gun.

11

Sullivan Unleashed

Sullivan, dressed and packing the .44 Automag and two boxes of shells, went to the roof. It had stopped snowing. He walked to the front of the building. Below, the firemen in their slickers and high boots were standing around outside the building, talking and laughing, some of them glancing up at the smashed-in window, probably assuming a gangland reprisal. Routine. Nothing much for them to do, now that they'd double-checked the place and removed everything that was smoldering. Three police cars were parked around the fire trucks. The street was clogged with official vehicles. He could hear the static-muffled, strangely detached voices coming from the radio speakers in the cops' patrol cars. There were people gathered on the sidewalk, some of them standing in bedroom slippers in two inches of snow, shifting from foot to foot for warmth and staring across the street. He looked across at the roof of the Belle Starr Hotel. He figured the guy had fired the projectile from there. He saw no one on the roof now. Of course.

Sullivan turned and walked across the roof to the next building. He went to the stair entrance. The door was locked. He had no patience for locked doors now. He kicked it in, and walked inside. Down the stairs, floor

after floor, and out onto the sidewalk, just as if he were a resident or a visitor to the building, coming out to see what all the fuss was about.

He crossed to the hotel and went inside. "Hi," he said to the dark-skinned man behind the desk. "Looking for a friend of mine. Silver-haired fellow."

"Oh, Mr. Crandall. Yes, he checked out just a few minutes ago."

"Crandall?" It wouldn't be his real name. All he knew about the guy was that he had silvery hair, and he'd been wearing a black raincoat when Sullivan had seen him. He hadn't gotten a close look at his face.

He considered bribing the clerk to let him into the assassin's room. But he knew "Crandall" would be too careful to have left anything behind.

He turned away and went out into the street.

M79 grenade launcher, Sullivan thought.

Not a cheap piece of equipment. Something Sullivan himself had used in Vietnam. Good ordnance. The guy had connections.

Sullivan walked to the corner. The staccato crackle of radio voices faded behind him. He stood on the corner and looked at Manhattan, one of the most dangerous cities in the country. And he wondered where to begin.

If he had to, he would start at one end of the island, and begin unraveling, like a man unraveling a whole sweater from a single thread.

The ambulance was gone. He'd seen the insignia on it. New York Hospital; that was at Sixty-eighth and York.

First he had to know whether he was going to avenge the living or the dead.

The emergency room was off-white and grimy around the edges. A TV in a ceiling rack blared about the weather, some newsman blandly asserting that it was unusual to get snow so early in the year, as if New York needed to be told. The plastic molded chairs lined up in the waiting area beside the triage station were filled.

There were a dozen or so unclassifiable people who mostly seemed no more concerned than if they were waiting in a doctor's office for a routine yearly checkup. A few others rocked in their seats, in pain or pretending to be. An old woman sat doddering in a wheelchair, now and then querulously asking the nurse why she hadn't been called.

Sullivan paced in the hallway beside the waiting area. The security guard looked at him, frowning, as if trying to remember if there was a rule against pacing in the hallway, and wishing that, if no rule existed, he could institute one.

Sullivan was realizing he had made a mistake.

The assassin would have left the scene, yes. But by now he would have returned to check on his kill. Probably wander casually up to some of the bystanders, ask how many people had been hurt in the explosion.

"A girl was hurt," they'd say. "They took her to the hospital."

"Oh, really?" he'd say. "I heard a rumor there was a man hurt too."

"No, just the one girl."

One way or another, he'd have come back to check. If Sullivan had waited around, he'd have seen him. Could have followed him. Could have killed him.

But it was too late now. Now the guy would know that Sullivan had survived. He would want to find Sullivan, to try again, or he would give it up, leave the city.

Don't give up, Sullivan thought. Try again. Just try it.

There must be a way to make him try again—on Sullivan's terms. Give him his chance, and then take it away from him.

The outside door burst open; three men came in, two of them holding up the third between them. The one they held between them was masked in blood, an ugly gash across his forehead slowly oozing red. He looked drunk. Concussion, probably a car wreck, Sullivan figured.

The triage nurse glanced at the new patient and saw he took priority. She called attendants; they put the man on a gurney and wheeled him through the double doors into the examination room.

A sallow-faced young woman hugged her belly, rocked in her chair, muttering, "He's no worse off than me. How come he goes in first?" The hospital staff ignored her.

A tall black nurse came out of the examination area. "Mr. Stark?" she called.

Sullivan strode up to her. "That's me."

"Your friend is hanging in there. But she's on the critical list. We're moving her upstairs. She's in a coma. Some kind of fragment from the explosion is pressing against her spine. They're going to operate as soon as possible. Okay?"

No, it was not okay. Sullivan felt helpless, but he said, "Okay."

"What caused the explosion?"

"A bomb. A kind of hand grenade. She was investigating some people, and the people she was investigating didn't like her doing her job so well."

The nurse sighed. "Ain't that a bitch. Always the good people who get hurt."

She turned away, then turned back as if remembering something. "Oh—there are some policemen in there. They came from the front way, I guess they didn't see you. They wanted to talk to somebody who knew her."

"Uh-huh. I have to make a call. I'll be right in to talk to them."

"I'll tell them." She went back into the exam room.

He turned and walked out the door. She's going to live, he thought urgently, willing it to come true. She's going to live.

Sullivan walked across the snowy driveway. The snow was slashed with tire tracks.

He paused at the corner, lit a cigarette, pulled his

coat more closely around him, and stepped out into the wind.

You bastard, he thought, you'll pay. *You'll pay!*

When Sullivan got back to the apartment building, intending to interrogate the three creeps chained up in the basement, the police and fire trucks had already gone. The samples had been taken from the blown room, the photos had been snapped, the tenants questioned. A certain Detective Krinsky had gone through the motions of asking the questions.

Krinsky had cleared the thing up quickly. A former lover, in the detective's opinion, had planted a bomb in the girl's room, in an act of revenge. She'd jilted him, Krinsky had asserted.

Moreland told Sullivan about it over a cup of instant coffee in Moreland's kitchenette. "I told him he was full of shit. I told him it was Legion. But he got this superior look and said, 'Leave the police work to the police.' I guess you're right about him. I heard him talking to reporters. He theorizes that the bomber may have been a man known to have associated with the victim. A wanted man. Jack Sullivan. The Specialist."

Sullivan looked out the window into the black night and laughed softly and bitterly. He drank off the tepid dregs of his coffee and stood. "I'm going to have a talk with your basement pets."

Moreland shook his head, and looked a little sheepish. "We let them go."

"What!"

"When the cops came we were afraid they'd look down there. I don't know why they would, but we were afraid they'd snoop through the whole building. We figured we'd get in trouble for keeping them chained up. We let them go. They walked out. Naturally they didn't complain to the cops."

Sullivan shrugged. "They probably wouldn't have known anything useful. I guess I'll just go and talk to somebody who does."

Sullivan went once more into the night. His stomach burned with the acrid instant coffee. The rage burned in him too, in his loins and his heart and his brain; he seemed to feel it tingling in the muscles of his jaw and the tendons of his fists. But he was calm now.

Look at a bomb before it explodes. It just sits there.

A little while later, Sullivan was sitting, calmly, immobile, nothing moving but his eyes. He was sitting in his van, which he'd taken out of its garage in preparation for his mission. He was staring at the front door of the Thirteenth Precinct stationhouse. He glanced at his watch. Krinsky would get off work soon. One A.M., they'd told him.

He waited and watched. At ten minutes to one a medium-sized man in a stiff-looking brown suit came out of the station and crossed quickly to his car. It was a Mercedes-Benz. Sullivan recognized him from Moreland's description. Crewcut blond hair, blond eyebrows, Slavic features, long nose.

The Mercedes started and pulled out of its slot, drove out into the street. The street had been swept of snow and sown with gravel. Sullivan started the van and followed.

A Mercedes. Didn't anybody wonder how Krinsky could afford a Mercedes on a detective's pay? He probably had his excuses. His family had given it to him, say. They were wealthy.

Krinsky drove west, across town to the West Side Highway. Sullivan pulled onto the highway behind him. Then Krinsky went south, and took the Holland Tunnel to Jersey City.

Sullivan was right behind him.

The detective drove out toward Hoboken, turned off into a suburb called Crustville. Sullivan pulled off with him.

Krinsky drove down a highway skirting the town, and into an industrial park. On the other side of the industrial park was a housing development, where he lived.

Sullivan waited till they were midway into the industrial park. To either side of the street were tall, enigmatic cylinders of black metal, squat warehouse buildings, crates and piles of scrap metal. The park was deserted now, except for a few night watchmen, each in his respective office watching late-night TV or sleeping.

Sullivan swerved into the left lane and accelerated, quickly catching up with the Mercedes.

"Shame to damage such a nice car, you crud," he muttered between clenched teeth as he slammed the armored fenders of the van sideways into the sportscar. He slammed it hard, and it only took once: the Mercedes ran off the road and piled into a ditch. Its engine snorted and died. Its lights still burned, illuminating a corner of the road that no one wanted to see clearly, spotlighting paper bags from fast-food eateries.

Sullivan did a U turn, came around behind the Mercedes, did another U, and drove at the man getting out of the little car.

Krinsky had a gun in his hand. But, as Sullivan expected, when he saw the big gray GMC van burning toward him he panicked. He turned and ran, then fell into the snow-filled ditch, wallowing desperately to get across, trying to reach a single light in the window of a watchman's office, forty yards across the parking lot.

Sullivan laughed. He gunned ahead, swerved into the parking lot, and stopped the van abruptly so it slid sideways, blocking Krinsky's escape.

Krinsky raised the gun and fired. The bullets *whanged* off the van's armored body. Sullivan drew the .44 and got out on the opposite side. He ran around to the rear corner of the van, and propped an arm on the metal, aiming the gun at Krinsky. The corrupt cop was thirty feet away.

"Throw the gun down, you sell-out bastard!" Sullivan shouted. His breath was visible like dragon's smoke in the cold air. "Now!"

Sullivan had the sights of the .44 trained on Krinsky's terrified face. He wanted to kill him.

He wanted to pull the trigger and blow the bastard away right there. Because he was part of the pattern, part of an evil link that had maimed Bonnie.

But he couldn't do it. He needed Krinsky alive.

"Who . . . who are you?"

"I'm your worst nightmare, you motherfucker!" Sullivan shouted. The words burst out of him, of their own volition. "I'm an honest man with a gun and a sense of justice, and I know what you deserve! Drop the gun or you'll get it here and now!"

Krinsky threw the gun into the snow.

"Now, get out of the ditch and come over to the van!"

Krinsky, gasping with fear, scrambled out of the ditch, his suit and hands caked with snow. He staggered to the van.

"Lean against it, legs apart, weight on your hands. You know the drill!"

Krinsky did as he was told, leaning on the side of the van.

Sullivan went to him, patting him down to be sure he didn't carry a small backup gun. He turned to the Mercedes.

He put four rounds into the car, blowing up the engine, smashing out the windshield, exploding the front tires. Mostly because he had to shoot something. Krinsky whimpered at the gunshots, squeezing his eyes shut.

"Some big brave cop you are," Sullivan snarled, kicking Krinsky's legs out from under him. Krinsky fell in the snow, yelping.

Sullivan dragged him to his feet by his collar, slammed him a few times against the van to be sure he was softened up, and then dragged him around to the back. He found Krinsky's cuffs, and cuffed him with them, hands behind his back. He opened the back of the van and shoved the cop in like he was a side of beef. Krinsky fell onto the empty metal floor with a grunt. Blood ran from his nose. His eye was swelling up.

Sullivan slammed the doors and went around to the front of the van, got in, and drove away.

Sullivan stood over Krinsky, his hands dripping blood. "I told you everything I know," Krinsky said in a strangled voice. He was lying on his side, doubled up in a fetal position. His face looked pulpy.

They were in Sullivan's cabin. Although he had abandoned it for months, Sullivan still owned it. For a while the FBI had watched it waiting for him to come back. Then Sullivan's contact at the agency, Sanson, convinced them it was a waste of time. Sullivan would never be stupid enough to return. They'd called off the surveillance. The place had been vandalized. The furnishings had been ripped out. Graffiti slashed jaggedly across the walls. The electricity had been turned off— Sullivan was conducting his interrogation by candlelight. It was cold in the room. The fireplace, near Krinsky, was cold and black. Sullivan and Krinsky had kept warm with exercise.

"Please . . ." Krinsky said, coughing. "Please."

"How many people are dead because you turned your back for money?" Sullivan said. "And you plead to me?"

He reached down and turned off the cassette tape recorder that had taken Krinsky's confession. The recording alone wouldn't be enough to convict Krinsky, since it had been illegally obtained, and would be called invalid by reason of coercion. But Krinsky's confession had named names, had connected the dots, and colored it all in. The department would know it was the truth, once they checked out those connections. They'd start hauling people in and asking about Krinsky; they'd find evidence, once they knew where to look.

"I'm not going to kill you, Krinsky," Sullivan said. "Because maybe once you were a real cop. Now you're a bogus cop. But you can live, and you'd better start running. Because this tape is going to the department's internal-affairs people. I got a friend in the feds who'll

get it to the right guys. Your ass is in a sling, Krinsky.
So leave the state. See how far you run before they pick
you up. And don't tell any more lies about me. If you
do, if you don't retract that bullshit about the Specialist,
I'll find you and I'll feed you into a meat grinder, inch by
inch." He grabbed a handful of Krinsky's hair and
jerked his head up, making him look him in the eye.
"You believe me?"

"I . . . I believe you." He spat out a tooth. "I'll retract
it, I swear. Just don't come near me again."

Sullivan let Krinsky's head fall to the floor. He
picked up the cassette, straightened, and looked down
at the man for a moment. He had earlier taken off
the cuffs. He couldn't beat a man who was wearing
handcuffs.

Sullivan turned on his heel and walked out. He walked
down the hill, got into the van, and drove it out onto
the snowy road. It slipped now and then, but it got him
into town.

Once in Manhattan, Sullivan stopped off at a phone
booth and called the hospital. He was told that Bonnie's
condition had improved, but she was still in danger.
They'd operated. She was still unconscious.

He went to the van. He sat in the dark, quiet car
for a moment, listening to the engine ticking to itself
as it cooled. Then he opened the glove compartment,
and found an envelope, a scrap of paper, and a pen.
On the scrap of paper he wrote: "Sanson—Make a
copy of this and then get it to NYPD Internal Affairs.
It's Authentic. Realize it's not admissible but the
names and arrangments detailed here can be followed
up on. He's probably already on the run. Will contact
you again shortly." He signed it, "Jack." He put the
note and the cassette tape in the envelope and sealed
it.

He addressed it to Special Agent Sanson, FBI HQ,
NYC. He drove to the Justice Department headquarters
and left it with the night guard at the front desk. The

guard stared after him, then stared at the envelope, wondering if it contained a bomb.

Sullivan walked out, climbed into the van, and drove back to New Jersey.

He had some serious ass-kicking to do out there.

12
Against the Odds

Krinsky had named names, and Sullivan had them.

And Krinsky had given him an address. The house of the Gonzales brothers. Hector, Jesus, and Jose Gonzales worked for Crackwell, now and then. They were his contact with the gangs Legion had hired to terrorize the tenants.

Krinsky had told Sullivan that Legion had left the country. He was in Sicily. Would be there for weeks. Very well. Before this mission was over, Jack Sullivan, too, would be in Sicily.

But first he had to deal with Fabrizzio.

Krinsky had given him that name too. But after knocking out a handful of Krinsky's teeth, breaking his collarbone and staving in a few ribs, Sullivan had come to the conclusion that Krinsky was telling the truth when he insisted he didn't know where Fabrizzio could be found. Or where Crackwell could be found. Krinsky's contact with Crackwell was through Hector Gonzales.

So Sullivan was going to politely ask Gonzales where Fabrizzio could be found.

Or maybe he would dispense with formalities. Maybe he'd do it another way. Yeah.

Yeah, he felt like doing it the hard way.

* * *

The Gonzales brothers lived in a renovated Victorian building. Brick-fronted with an old-fashioned facade, it was squeezed in between two others identical except for the color of their window-frame trimming. Not a gang hangout. This was home. Sullivan would have to be careful not to hurt the civilians.

He was being careful with himself. Trying to rein himself in. But it was hard to keep the boiling rage in check.

He pulled up across the street and looked up at the building. Lights on the top floor. Sullivan parked and crossed the street, rang the buzzer in the code Krinsky had given him—two longs, two shorts, and a long. He heard a buzzing as they unlocked the door from above. He opened it and went in, climbing the stairs to the top floor. Someone looked out at him through the peephole in the door. "Who zat?" someone asked.

"My name's Richie," Sullivan shouted. "Krinsky sent me."

"What you want?"

"You hear what happened to Carlos Ajidas?"

"Yeah, we hear zat."

"Well, I'm his replacement! I got some money to deliver for Mr. Crackwell!"

The door opened. "You shouldn't say stuff like that loud in the hall, man," said the man in the doorway.

Sullivan shrugged and stepped inside, shouldering brusquely past the man.

"Why you bringing it here, man? That ain't the usual way he do it."

Sullivan said, "Just following orders."

There was an old woman sitting in an easy chair, its arms covered with doilies. She was watching a Spanish station on TV. A Spanish comedian in an absurd checkered hat capered on the screen. The old woman giggled. Beside her, in a rocking chair, an old man slept with his mouth ajar, a copy of *El Diario* on his lap. There was a plastic cover on each article of furniture, except on the wooden kitchen chairs.

Three Hispanic men sat around a kitchen table, playing poker. Only, now they were looking at Sullivan, sizing him up. Sullivan could have been one of Legion's hardmen. He had the stature, and the scarred face helped.

"Yo, check out Al Pacino. Scarface, man," said one of the men at the table.

The other guys laughed.

Sullivan smiled. "Which one's Hector?" he asked.

The one who'd let him in said, "Right here." He was a short but muscular man, wearing a sleeveless shirt to emphasize his brawn. He had a small black mustache and a bony face.

"Need to talk to you outside," Sullivan said, glancing at the old woman.

"We can talk here."

Sullivan shook his head. "Outside."

"You want to give me the money on the street?"

"In the hallway."

"But—"

"You want to keep working for Mr. Crackwell?"

Hector shrugged. "Okay." He spoke in Spanish to the guys at the table. They nodded.

Sullivan went out into the hall, and Hector followed. Sullivan went down the stairs.

"Hey, how come we got to go down downstairs?" Hector asked, closing the door.

Sullivan didn't answer. He continued downward.

He waited for Hector in the hallway of the first floor. Hector came down, complaining, and turned the corner around the banister post. As he rounded the corner, he met Sullivan's fist. He doubled over, gasping, as Sullivan's slug displaced the air in the pit of his stomach.

Sullivan stepped behind him and kicked. Hector went over on his face.

Sullivan pulled the .44 and pressed it to the back of Hector's head. "You want to know who killed Carlos Ajidas, man?" Sullivan asked. "It was me. My name's Jack Sullivan. I'm the one they call the Specialist. You ever heard of me?"

"Yeah, yeah. I heard," Hector said in a high voice like a vacuum cleaner starting up as he tried to get his breath. He lay on his side, clutching his gut.

Sullivan took a piece of paper from his pocket and tucked it in the back pocket of Hector's pants. "You get this message to Crackwell, tell him it's for Fabrizzio. It's an address. The address of where I'll be tomorrow night, midnight—if Fabrizzio wants to get the job done. You understand?"

"I understand. Take off the gun, man. You didn't have to do all this shit, I'd have given him the message without you pushing me around."

"Oh, I know that, Hector. I didn't hit you so you'd give him the message. I hit you because you're a dope-pushing scumbag. I should kill you, except who would carry the message then?"

Sullivan straightened and holstered the gun. He left the building, crossed the street, got into the van, started it up, and drove away.

Back in Manhattan, Sullivan called the hospital again. No change in Bonnie's condition.

Sullivan went to an Irish bar to get drunk. At an Irish bar, the bartender never tells you you've had enough.

It was a sour-smelling place with a slanting wooden floor. The more he drank, the more slanted the floor seemed. He drank Irish whiskey with a beer chaser.

He wondered. Why challenge Fabrizzio the way he had? Why not just hunt him down? Why do it the hard way? Because he was mad, mad as hell, and he had to take it out on someone who deserved it. But was he maybe even madder at himself? Maybe blaming himself because Bonnie had gotten hurt? He should know better than to let someone get close to him. Especially when there was a contract out on him. He should have stayed away from her, except for the necessary business contacts.

But he needed her.

No. No, Jack Sullivan was legendary for his toughness. A tough guy doesn't need anyone.

Does he?

Sullivan polished off two-thirds of a fifth, staggered to the nearest hotel, and fell into a sleep haunted by morbid dreams.

He woke at eleven the next morning. He opened his eyes, and immediately regretted it.

Filtered through the overcast, the sunlight was anemic. But even that dim light hurt his eyes like hot irons. He blinked. Felt like he had sand under his eyelids. His tongue was like the inner soles of a jogger's shoes when he's ready to throw them away.

He got up, and winced. His head hurt, he was dizzy, and his stomach hated its own existence. He showered, using first hot and then icy cold water. He dressed and went downstairs to a grocery store, and found a small jar of cayenne pepper in the spices section. He bought the cayenne and went to a coffee shop, ordered fresh-squeezed orange juice, toast, and coffee. Sitting at the counter, he ate the toast, then dumped about two table-spoons of the cayenne pepper into his orange juice. The Greek waiter stared at him, gaping so his toothpick fell out of his mouth.

Sullivan stirred the cayenne pepper into the orange juice, took a deep breath, and swigged the whole mixture down, the entire glass all at once. He set the glass down with a clack and gripped the edges of the counter.

The world rocked. In various locations around the planet, volcanoes erupted. Sullivan was sure of that fact: he could feel them going off in his stomach. He felt a series of hot and cold flashes, and the room seemed to spin.

Without having to be asked, the waiter brought him a large glass of water. Sullivan drank it down and asked for another one. He took a bottle of B vitamins from his coat pocket and swallowed two of them with the second glass of water.

And after a few minutes he felt a lot better.

"What the hell you doing, buddy?" the Greek waiter asked, inserting another toothpick in his mouth.

"Cure for hangovers," Sullivan said. "Cayenne pepper. Works good. B vitamins and lots of water. Half of a hangover is dehydration."

Sullivan felt ready to eat something. He ordered an omelet, ate it, drank his coffee, and then he noticed that a guy at the other end of the counter was staring at him. He was a middle-aged man, clean-shaven, wearing a tired gray suit. Sullivan didn't like the look the guy was giving him.

It was a look of recognition.

A cop, maybe. Sullivan tossed a five-dollar bill onto the counter, got up, and walked outside, not too quickly. It was cool but sunny. The snow was melting.

He crossed the slushy street to his van. As he was unlocking it, he glanced over his shoulder at the coffee shop. The gray-suited man was using the restaurant's pay phone.

Sullivan got into the van, started it, began to pull out, and stopped. A beer truck had pulled up and double-parked beside him. The driver was nowhere in sight.

Sullivan looked at the sidewalk. A parking meter and a steel trash bin blocked his van. He couldn't pull onto the sidewalk.

Thinking: *The cops'll be here any minute*, Sullivan got out of the van. Maybe he should abandon it. But he'd need it tonight.

Sullivan went over to the beer truck and looked inside. The keys were in the ignition. Sullivan climbed in, started the engine, and pulled it up about thirty feet. He got out. A large, big-gutted florid-faced man was glaring at him, tapping a long-necked beer bottle into his palm.

Sullivan said, "Fuck with me and I'll kill you."

It was the tone—not the words—that did it. The truck driver's eyes widened. He backed away.

Sullivan went around the front of the truck, and climbed into the van. He was not in a good mood.

Sullivan drove to the corner. The traffic blocked his way. A gridlock had formed at the intersection. He looked into the outside rearview mirror, expecting to see police cars screaming around the corner. Nothing yet.

But someone knocked on the window of the passenger-side door.

Sullivan looked over. It was Sanson. Sanson from the FBI.

Sanson and Sullivan were standing at the railing in the riverside park, looking out at the East River. A tugboat, painted in bright reds and yellows, chugged by, making a widening V of wake in the broad expanse of green water. In a few seconds, the waves from the tugboat's wake sloshed against the concrete wall below the railing.

Sanson was smoking a pipe; Sullivan finished a Lucky Strike. They hadn't spoken in a while.

"So you're not going to give it up," Sanson said.

Sullivan shook his head.

"You sure you know who fired that grenade, Jack?" Sanson continued. "Lot of people have it in for you. They're standing in line to throw grenades at you."

"I've confirmed my information."

"Through Krinsky?"

"Yeah, before I recorded him."

"We can't help you on this one, Jack," Sanson said. He finished his pipe and tapped it out on the railing. The breeze caught the ashes and swirled them out over the river.

"That's the way I want it," Sullivan said, flicking the butt of his cigarette into the water.

"That's a bad habit you've got pal, working alone. Listen, you don't fuck up our investigation, you hear?"

Sullivan nodded.

Sanson said, "What about that job we talked about?"

"You tell me. You set it up the way I asked for?"

"Yeah. You're completely independent. If the government offers you a job, you don't have to take it unless you want to. You're the head of the team. We're calling it Project Scapel. You'll have to give us a full report, but otherwise you're in complete control of each operation. And, Jack—we're going out on a limb for you. After that wild-west shotout of yours with Toscani . . . Christ, I needed a calculator to keep track of the bodies."

"Speak plainly," Sullivan said.

"Plainly, you kill only the enemy you *have* to kill. The rest you capture or you leave to us to pursue. If you take the commando team on, you don't go on vendettas. You get the job done. Do it your way, as long as it's professional."

Sullivan said, "If I take the job, that's the way it'll be."

Sanson nodded. "Okay. Try to keep a low profile on this thing with Legion. Now, we're waiting to get the budget approved for the commando team. Take a few months. We'll be ready to move on this in March. We're counting on you, Jack. I'll keep you posted through that post-office-box number you gave me."

They shook hands, and Sanson walked back through the park to the street.

Sullivan stood alone awhile at the railing, looking at the river, watching the sunlight gleam off the waves.

Flushing, Queens. Eleven-thirty P.M. A parking structure, five stories, no longer in use. Condemned by the city. Whole damn thing might fall down on me before I get Fabrizzio, Sullivan thought, sizing up the building.

The parking structure was an abandoned dark hulk set amid a neighborhood of stores, warehouses, and restaurants—all of them closed now. The street was not a main drag, and no cars passed. An elevated subway train ran behind the parking structure, thundering at the empty building as it wended through the city.

Sullivan had gone against his common sense, his own experience, his standard technique. He had told the enemy where he would be, and he had not gone there ahead of time to set traps. He had not staked out the place to see what Fabrizzio would set up. He had let Fabrizzio go in first.

It wasn't the right way to do it. It was the defiant way.

Let Fabrizzio set up any way he wanted. Let him bring an army in with him. It wasn't going to help him. And Sullivan wanted it to be difficult. He wanted the odds against him. It wasn't professional to want that. It was, maybe, a kind of penance.

Sullivan stood across the street from the building. He had a nylon bag slung over one shoulder. It contained an Ingram Mac 10 machine pistol. He had four clips for it. In his leather flight jacket was the .44 Automag.

Sullivan opened his nylon bag and took out the Ingram. It was a blocky gun, like a handgun trying to pass itself off as a machine gun, with a long clip jutting under the grip.

Sullivan turned and walked to his van. He got in, laid the Ingram across his lap, and started the van. He drove it across the street and into the cavelike darkness of the parking structure.

He switched on the van's lights.

I'm coming, you bastard, he thought. *You'd better be ready.*

Fabrizzio was ready. The first three levels of the parking structure had been booby-trapped. On the fifth floor, four thugs were poised to catch Sullivan in a crossfire. On the roof, Fabrizzio waited with the 30.06 and the three Gonzales brothers as backup.

"I wish you'd let us wait for him downstairs," Jesus Gonzales said, hefting the sawed-off shotgun in his hand. "I want to kill him. He pulled that shit on Hector."

"You may get your chance," Fabrizzio said. "He's not a man easily stopped, but one way or another, we'll stop him. To live through this night, he'd have to be a one-man army."

13

Explosions

Sullivan's van was not what it appeared to be. It eased the odds against him a bit.

Its body was custom armored. The windshield was bullet-resistant. And inside, under the dashboard, was a small rocket launcher, which he'd recently modified to carry a 20mm round. There was a round in it, ready to fire. The side doors housed steel-shuttered firing slits. As he drove slowly up the ramp, he pulled a lever, and steel shields emerged to cover the wheels.

Sullivan himself was armored. He wore a standard bullet-proof vest under his coat. It wouldn't stop every kind of round. It would be effective against most pistols. But it wouldn't do a damn thing to protect his head.

The odds were against Sullivan, and he knew it.

The ramps spiraled up into the parking structure like the interior of a seashell. A little light from a streetlamp poured in near the roof, on the left, where the walls ended in a metal grille for ventilation. But most of the interior was dark, cavernous, echoey, scored with graffiti and littered here and there with heaps of trash, where people had dumped their refuse, and where gangs now and then had held their "social events," like gang-bangs. He passed more than one rotting mattress on the ramp leading to the second floor. On the second level, he stopped the van with jarring suddenness.

There was just the faintest suggestion of a horizontal line in the air about three feet ahead of his van's grille. A thin black line in the headlights about shin level. He put on the emergency brake. Ingram in hand, he got out of the van. He crouched for a moment, looking around. No movement. Nothing except that black line in the air to warn him all was not as it seemed.

He circled behind the van, crept up on the other side, and found the wire. It ran low to the far wall. He traced it back. In an old iron bedspring, he found it: a Claymore mine. It was set up to blast across the ramp, sending its antipersonnel pellets out in a horizontal spray. The trip wire Sullivan discovered would've set it off.

He went back to the van and backed it up about twenty feet, just outside the Claymore's main cone of fire. He switched off the lights, took a small flashlight from the glove compartment, and got out of the van. He traced the wire to the left-hand wall, and found the bolt it was attached to. Very carefully—very, very carefully—he untied the wire from the bolt and slackened it. He let out a long relieved breath when he got it loose without triggering the mine.

Sullivan carried the loosened end of the wire back toward the van. He crouched behind the van, the bulk of the vehicle between him and the mine, and pulled the wire.

The Claymore blew, roaring out fire and sending a murderous hailstorm of steel pellets into the air, most of them smacking into the concrete of the far side of the garage, some of them rebounding, ricocheting with a *zing*, a few more rattling off the hide of the van.

The echoes of the blast died away. The smoke drifted off.

Sullivan let out a yell of pain, and a long series of curses, ending in a despairing gurgle.

But he was completely unhurt.

He waited.

He heard voices, men talking excitedly, bootsteps clapping down the ramp.

"Hold it, goddammit, Hank, you can't be sure—"

"You heard that yell, we got the bastard!" the other man replied. They came around the curve of the ramp, one a little ahead of the other, trotting with M16's in their hands.

They slowed when they came to the blast zone, their eyes on the ground, looking for Sullivan's corpse.

Then Hank looked up and saw the van. "Hey, what the fuck—" he began.

The other one opened up at the van. M16 rounds rebounded deafeningly off the grille, knocking out one of the headlights. He ended his burst, and then Sullivan stepped out from behind the van and raked back and forth with the chattering Ingram, the dark spaces of the garage lighting up with the strobing muzzle flashes, 9mm tumblers whizzing to rip the two men apart, spinning them around screaming. He expended a clip on them. They lay still. He ejected the clip, reached into the van, took out a fresh one, and slapped it into place. He waited.

No one else came. They'd figured it out.

Sullivan got into the van, set the Ingram on his lap, quietly closed the door, and drove slowly up the ramp, the light from his single remaining beam sweeping over the spreading pool of blood around his victims as he took the corner.

The van rolled on—and the right-front wheel dipped, the van lurched, and ground to a stop. Sullivan put it in park. He got out, carrying the Ingram. There was an eight-foot-wide hole in the concrete floor, between two heaps of trash. Fabrizzio had covered it with a broad flap of cardboard supported by two thin sticks of balsa wood. They'd expected him to walk through here, and fall, probably break his neck below. The van was only one wheel into the hole—he had approached it at an angle. He cleared a space in the trash to the right, just big enough for the van to squeeze through. He backed the van up, switching into four-wheel-drive to pull it from the hole, and drove around the trap.

On the next level he didn't see the booby-trap trigger. The van struck it, whatever it was, and two shotguns mounted in brackets near the ceiling went off, one on either side. Shotgun pellets whined off the van; one clump struck the windshield, webbing it in the upper-left-hand corner, but not breaking through. If he'd been on foot, he'd have been torn apart.

He kept going, up to the next level. . . .

Gunfire erupted from both sides of the ramp. Two high heaps of junk were arranged like bunkers on the left and right of the path; the one on the right fired from behind an iron barrel and bales of old newspaper. Assault-rifle rounds smashed into the windshield, and the bullets were too heavy for the glass to resist. The windows shattered inward, rounds whistled past to ricochet inside the rear of the van.

Sullivan hit the brake, ducked down, and cranked the rocket launcher into position. A panel in the nose of the van slid open; the launcher muzzle emerged. The van was already angled toward one of the gunmen. He approximated the firing line, and threw the switch that launched the rocket.

The round sped out, angling slightly upward, streaming rocket exhaust; it impacted with the iron barrel. The van rocked with the explosion; the garage echoed with it. New cracks appeared in the walls. A chunk of ceiling fell down amid shrapnel and bits of debris and smoke, and one more assassin was sent express special delivery to hell.

Sullivan drew the .44 and, sliding the firing slit open and crouching below window level, he opened up on the left-side gunman. He fired through the smoke at the exposed corner of the man's head glimpsed above the muzzle flash. Sullivan heard a muffled shriek, and the man fell from sight. Sullivan waited. There was no more gunfire. But he knew it wasn't over yet. He drove off, and the night air, rank with the smell of garbage and mildewy concrete, streamed in through the shattered windshield.

He drove up to the top, thinking he'd passed all the booby traps—and the van struck a mine, this one hidden under a heap of rags on the van's blind side.

Sullivan felt a brutal shock wave and a flash of light, and then a giant's hand smacked him out of his seat. He flew against the passenger-side door; the window glass was shattered by his shoulder: The pane of his consciousness shattered, too. Darkness closed in on him.

It was a red darkness. An angry red. It faded to a lighter red, then orange, then yellow blobbed with orange, and then he opened his eyes. To his surprise, he found he was still among the living.

He was being dragged along the ramp, a man on either side supporting him with a hand under each armpit. His arms hung limply, his head was bowed. He kept it that way, instinctively playing dead, opening his eyes only a crack, letting his feet drag on the concrete. Gathering his strength. His head rang like a gong from the blast. He was still half-stunned, but he felt no pain except for a headache. The van had taken the brunt of the blast.

He peered left, through his eyelashes, and saw his .44 swing by in the left hand of one of the hardmen.

"Yo, thas a nice shootin' iron, man, you gonna keep that thing, man?" the one on the right asked.

"Chure, he owes me that, man," the other replied. Sullivan recognized the voice. Hector Gonzales. "You know what that is? A .44 Automag." Gonzales said something more, but it was in Spanish. Like many Puerto Ricans in the New York area, they spoke a mixture of English and Spanish with one another.

Then the dragging stopped. Sullivan heard Hector speak. "I think he's still alive, Tony."

Tony? Tony "The Chill" Fabrizzio. Sullivan was within a few feet of the man who'd put Bonnie in the hospital.

But still he played possum, letting strength seep back into him, waiting for his chance.

"Still alive?" Fabrizzio said. " Good!" There was elation in his voice. Sullivan heard the click of a rifle being cocked. "I want to finish him personally. But I want him to be awake when I do it."

He turned to a figure behind him. Sullivan could tell he was looking away because his voice came to him indirectly. "Jose, get me that canteen—we'll see if we can wake our guest up for the execution."

As Fabrizzio spoke, Sullivan was slowly bending his knees, cocking his legs under him. Hector noticed it and started to shout—

Just as Sullivan got his feet under him and sprang.

He leapt left, onto Hector, knocking him down, one hand closing over the .44, at the same time twisting Hector's body to shield him from his brothers and Fabrizzio.

Sullivan fell on his back, Hector atop him, facing down, struggling.

But now Sullivan had the .44 and he fired, lying on his back shooting up at the three other men. Jesus Gonzales took a round in the throat; at that range it nearly blew his head off his shoulders. He flopped backward, dead before he hit the ground. Jose was struggling with Fabrizzio, who was trying to level his rifle at the two struggling men.

"No, you'll hit my brother, you bastard!"

He wrenched the rifle from Fabrizzio. Fabrizzio turned to run.

Jose was in the way. Sullivan squeezed off two shots, and Jose went down with a round through each lung. Hector's hands were around Sullivan's throat, tightening. His face, livid with fury, stared down at him from above, teeth bared, like a demon mask. Sullivan brought the .44 between them and blew away the top of Hector's skull, sending his brains into the air in a shower of red and gray.

Sullivan rolled the corpse off him. He stood shakily,

looking for Fabrizzio. They were on the roof. There was a rope ladder hooked over a concrete barrier. Sullivan strode unsteadily to it and looked over the side. It ran down to the next level, where there was a gap in the ventilation grating. Fabrizzio was nowhere to be seen. He had left himself an exit, just in case Sullivan had got this far. He'd gone down to the level just below and by now he was nearly down to the street. Sirens howled in the distance, coming nearer. Someone had reported the explosions.

Sullivan was dizzy, blood-soaked, and tired. But he turned and staggered down the ramp, picking up speed on the downhill slope, trying to catch up with Fabrizzio.

He passed the burning wreckage of his van, looked at it ruefully, and kept going. Now and then he poked through the trash heaps, hoping to find Fabrizzio hiding somewhere along the way. No such luck.

Sullivan hurried onward, pacing himself, beginning to get his legs back, his coordination returning, adrenaline pumping strength into him. And the kill fury rose up in him. The bastard who'd put Bonnie in the hospital was getting away.

He reached street level and saw Fabrizzio turning the corner off to the west, running south. The sirens were approaching from the east. Sullivan crossed the street and ran after Fabrizzio. As he reached the corner, the police and fire vehicles came around behind him. Sullivan kept going. No one spotted him.

Sullivan ejected the clip from the gun, and found another in his coat pocket. He slapped it into the .44, and sprinted after Fabrizzio, who was hailing a cab on the far corner.

Fabrizzio got into the cab and it drove off.

Sullivan saw a lemon-colored Trans Am, its hood painted with the Trans Am eagle in gold and black, pull up at the light. He ran into the street, jerked the passenger door open, and slid in beside a startled teenager.

Sullivan pointed the gun at him and said, "See that cab? Follow it and *don't lose it*."

The boy had longish brown hair and a wispy, still-born mustache. He gaped at Sullivan through blue-tinted aviator glasses. He wore a T-shirt that read *Bullshirt*. There were fuzzy dice hanging in his rear window.

Sullivan wouldn't have shot the kid. But he knew that the kid didn't know that Sullivan wouldn't shoot him.

So the kid nodded and said, "Uh, okay, but he's way down the avenue already—"

"Go through the red light."

"What! I'll get busted!"

Sullivan raised the gun meaningfully. "Do it!"

The kid stepped on the accelerator and the car lurched ahead; the kid shifted upward, and traffic screeched around them. Then they were through the intersection, racing after the cab.

"What's your name, kid?" Sullivan asked.

"Mark Wishbone."

"No, seriously kid—"

"That's really my name."

"Then I'll call you Mark. Mark, can this baby shut down that cab?"

"Huh? Sure! Of course, man! She's supercharged!"

"Show me."

Mark accelerated, weaving in and out of traffic, gunning wildly down the road, beginning to enjoy himself. He raced through red lights, whipped the Trans Am out into the left lane, ignoring the solid double lines, breaking rules with abandon, knowing he could later blame it on the gunman.

The cab led them into Manhattan. They emerged from the tunnel under the river into the tunnel of the urban night. Islands of light flashed by. The cab slowed. Mark overtook it and raced past.

"What you doing, Mark!"

"I thought you wanted to shut 'em down?"

"I didn't mean it was a goddamn race. Now, turn around . . ."

They U-turned, the tires squealing, the centrifugal force wrenching them in their seats.

Fabrizzio was getting out of the cab, running across the sidewalk into a tall ivy-covered brownstone. It was an imposing building, with an elaborate black metal grillwork over the windows.

Fabrizzio vanished into the interior.

Sullivan shouted, "Pull up here!" Mark jerked the car to a stop and Sullivan leapt out.

"Hey!" Mark shouted. "What's this all about, anyway!"

"I'm a cop," Sullivan said, "and that guy didn't pay his traffic tickets."

Mark turned white.

Sullivan ran into the building—and stopped short in the lobby.

Two quarterback-size bruisers were standing in his way, a yard off, and one of them had a .32 in his hamlike hand. Both were wearing pressed blue suits, complete with little immaculately folded kerchiefs in the jacket pockets. The one on the left, with the gun, had a big pasty face, jowls, and tufted gray eyebrows. He was shaved bald. The other was a big black guy chewing a wooden match.

"The match doesn't go with the suit," Sullivan said.

"Drop the piece," the left-hand bruiser said.

"Okay," Sullivan said. "Don't get uptight. Catch." He tossed the .44 casually at the guy with the gun. He looked down to catch it, scowling in annoyance, and as he looked away, Sullivan's left hand chopped down on his beefy one, knocking the .32 from his hand. He jerked back in surprise. Both guns fell to the floor. The black guy lunged at Sullivan, but the Specialist had expected the move, was already sidestepping, grabbing the black bouncer by the shoulder and helping him on his way so that he ran head-on into the thick glass of the lobby doors. He grunted and fell to his hands and knees, stunned. The other one was swinging at Sullivan; Sullivan ducked, stepped inside and jabbed hard and short to the man's Adam's apple. He staggered back, gasping. Sullivan slammed him with a left uppercut and a right cross, and he went down.

Sullivan turned. The black guy was getting to his feet, but he was still half stooped over. Sullivan drop-kicked him, his steel-toed boot impacting hard with the point of the thug's jaw. Teeth crackled on teeth, and the guy stood up straight with the impact of the blow. He swayed, and fell over backward, out cold, spread-eagled on the tile.

Sullivan scooped up both guns. He slipped the .32 into his pocket, and the .44 into his jacket shoulder holster.

He looked around the mirrored lobby, musing on his next step.

One floor down was a basement casino, an illegal gambling establishment. Sullivan had been there once, looking for a contact when he was investigating Toscani. Fabrizzio had ties with the New York Mafia, the casino's owners. He figured they'd hide him. Sullivan wasn't so sure they would.

He made up his mind. He took the .32 from his pocket, and turned to the white bouncer, who was sitting up and shaking his head groggily.

Sullivan stepped behind him and pressed the gun to the back of his neck. "Get up," Sullivan said.

"You in big trouble, pal," the bouncer said. His voice was hoarse from the punch to the throat. He stood up, blinking, swaying.

"Shut up," Sullivan told him. "Move. We're going downstairs."

They walked to the elevator, and the bouncer pressed the button. The elevator came up, and let out three blond, giggling, mink-wrapped women with plunging necklines. Sullivan moved the gun down to the small of the bouncer's back, where they wouldn't see it. The debutantes fluttered by, hardly glancing at the two men, and went out to a waiting limousine.

The bouncer stepped into the elevator, Sullivan close behind him. Sullivan turned the bouncer around to face the doors, and moved around behind him. As they descended he said, "You're going to get me in. I want Fabrizzio. No one else'll be bothered. . . . Where do I find him?"

"He's probably in the office with Mr. Lozini," the bouncer said as they stepped off the elevator.

"Act natural," Sullivan said. He jabbed the barrel of the gun into the bouncer's kidney to emphasize the point.

There was a man sitting at a glass window a little ways down the carpeted hallway. Beside the window was a door of blond oak. The man behind the window had permed shoulder-length black hair and the standard-issue blue suit. "Going in with an old buddy of mine, Harold," the bouncer said.

"He ain't wearin' a tie," the man in the booth said.

He looked Sullivan over dubiously. Sullivan was disheveled, caked in spots with dried blood, but the doorman couldn't see most of the blood from where he sat. He saw only Sullivan's head, shoulders, and part of his chest.

Sullivan jabbed the gun into the bouncer's back. "He was in a little car mix-up," the bouncer said. "We're gonna clean him up, loan him one of our suits. He's got an appointment with Mr. Lozini."

Harold shrugged and pressed a button. There was a buzzing sound, signaling that the door was unlocked. The bouncer opened it and they went through. They were in an anteroom with a potted palm and a plush red rug. Muzak played from a ceiling speaker. Across the anteroom were swinging saloon doors. On one wing of the doors was the word *Good* and on the other was *Luck*. Beyond the saloon doors was the bustle and laughter and clatter and repetitive number-calling of the casino. "Office is to the right," the bouncer said. "Up those steps."

"Is there a back way out of that office?"

"Sure, Mr. Lozini has a back way out, in case of raids," the guard said sullenly.

"Let's go," Sullivan said. They crossed to the steps and went up the short flight. The bouncer opened the blondwood office door.

There were two men in the small office. One was Fabrizzio. The other was Lozini, Sullivan assumed. He was a squat white-haired man with a basset-hound sag to his face. He wore a white tuxedo and he had a white cigarette holder clenched in his teeth. "Okay, but just till the morning, Tony," he was saying. "We run a class act—"

He broke off, seeing Sullivan and the bouncer.

Fabrizzio turned and looked, and went pale.

Lozini stood, and there was a .45 automatic in his hand. He pointed it at Sullivan. "This little baby'll drill right through the dumbshit you brought in here," Lozini said. "And it'll get you too. And I couldn't miss at this range."

"Shoot him, Federico, for God's sake!" Fabrizzio said backing toward the door at the other side of the office.

Sullivan said, "Hold it, Fabrizzio."

Fabrizzio froze.

Sullivan turned to Lozini. "We start shooting, we'll both get it. You know that."

Lozini shrugged. "There's a good chance."

"Then give him to me. He's not your responsibility."

Lozini said, "I can't just hand him over. Not to the guy who killed Boss Toscani. Toscani and I, we were old-time associates. But on the other hand, I don't want no shooting here. I don't want this place to have that kind of roughneck reputation. So I'll tell you what I'll do. Fabrizzio goes through that door. We give him a thirty-second lead. You can go after him, and after that it's out of my hands."

Sullivan said, "Okay."

Lozini—looking at Sullivan but talking to Fabrizzio—said, "Tony, get out of here and if you live through this, don't come and lay your dead rats on my doormat no more."

"But, Federico, hey, this ain't right, this man is an enemy of the Family—"

"We got a truce with him. We don't fuck with him and he don't fuck with us. Legion, he's not one of our people. We tolerated him, he's got a few contacts, but he's not part of this thing of ours. I have made up my mind, Tony. Go, and . . ." He grinned wolfishly. "Good luck."

Fabrizzio snarled to himself, then turned and opened the door. He stepped through.

Lozini began to count to thirty.

Sullivan moved toward the door, keeping the bouncer between himself and Lozini.

When Lozini said, "Thirty!" Sullivan shoved the bouncer toward Lozini, opened the door, and ran outside.

He was in a narrow alley. Fabrizzio was nowhere to be seen.

Sullivan ran to the sidewalk and looked around.

No good. He was gone.

Sullivan put the .32 in his pocket. He stood like a statue on the street, watching the cars go by, his fists clenched. People walked by him, staring, wondering about this rumpled, scratched-up, bloodstained stranger with the ominous scars. They gave him a wide berth and hurried on.

Sullivan seethed with frustration. He'd almost had him. He had an urge to go back to the casino and take his frustration out on Lozini.

But that would be misdirected energy. Because he wasn't going to give up. He was going to get Fabrizzio.

He had an idea where he could find him.

14

To The Ends of the Earth— If Necessary, Even to Queens

Crackwell had been thinking. He had a problem on his hands: Fabrizzio. Fabrizzio had come to him asking for sanctuary. He was sitting tensely in the attic room of Legion's house right now, waiting for Crackwell to "arrange transportation" and get him out of town. But Crackwell had other plans.

He was in Legion's office, sitting at Legion's desk, thinking about Legion's money. For a long time he had been brooding on the inequities in his relationship with Legion. It seemed to Crackwell that he was taking most of the risks, dealing with the smugglers, the buyers, the cops he had to pay off, while Legion sat back and raked in the benefits. Crackwell wasn't getting a big enough slice.

Legion had left Crackwell in charge of overseeing this Fabrizzio-Sullivan hit. He had given him fifty grand in cash to pay Fabrizzio once the job was done. Only now it was beginning to look as if Fabrizzio wasn't up to the job. He was a skillful man, but he was essentially a coward, and this Sullivan had him spooked. Fabrizzio was sitting up in the attic, drinking gin and muttering that Sullivan was some kind of supernatural entity, something more than human, that he was impossible to shake, impossible to kill, that Sullivan was coming for him, and he must get far, far away.

So the problem was, how could he supervise a hit that just wasn't coming off?

Find another way to do it. That's right. And if he got rid of both Sullivan and Fabrizzio, he could keep the fifty thousand for himself. Tell Legion he had paid it to Fabrizzio. There was a way to get rid of both men, and no one would ever know what had become of Tony the Chill.

Crackwell picked up the phone and dialed a subordinate. Victor Esala. Esala's wife answered; Esala came on the line a moment later.

"Victor? Crackwell. You remember I called you and asked you could you get me a gang for rousting tenants and you suggested that bunch under the station? You still on good terms with their leader?"

Victor sighed. "He is my cousin, I'm sorry to say. He's crazy. That bunch, they are all crazy. They are like animals."

"Good."

When Sullivan got to the house, he was surprised to see the little man sitting on the front stoop waving to him. He was a wizened, goateed little man in a porkpie hat. He wore dark glasses—despite the fact that it was two in the morning.

Sullivan had gone to his hotel, showered, changed, and hired a car from the twenty-four-hour service. He told the driver to wait, and got out, walked up the path. He wondered if it were a setup. But he had a sense for those things. And he sensed that the house behind the little man was empty.

The small Hispanic smiled up at Sullivan, showing a gold tooth. "I am Victor," he said. "I have this to tell you from Crackwell. He is tired of this fight. He wants to give Fabrizzio to you, to make the peace, but he doesn't want it to be here. Everything must be quiet here. It is in Grand Central Station."

Sullivan stared. "What? Why there?"

Victor shrugged. "They tell Fabrizzio they are taking him to a train, which will take him to the airport. This train is at Grand Central."

Sullivan frowned. It sounded all wrong. Now he smelled the setup, though it was still a long way off.

Victor took a slip of paper from his pocket. "This is directions where to find Fabrizzio in that place." He handed the paper to Sullivan.

"Okay," Sullivan said, "I'll play along. And we'll see."

He went back to the car, got in, and told the driver, "Grand Central."

The driver started the car. Sullivan said, "Hold it a second."

He got out and went back to Victor, took him by the arm, dragged him around to the back of the house.

"Please!" Victor said. "I don't hurt you! Why you hurt me?"

"I'm not going to hurt you. I just want you where I can keep an eye on you. Come on." He kicked in the back door and began a search of the house, the .44 in his hand and Victor always a little in front of him.

"No one here!" Victor protested. "They all going with Mr. Crackwell and Fabrizzio. Everybody gone!"

"Who is everybody?"

"There are two bodyguards here, for Mr. Crackwell and Mr. Legion. They gone with Crackwell and Fabrizzio now. Mr. Legion, he's not in the city any more."

Sullivan searched the place top and bottom. In the attic he found a glass half-full of gin and beside it, several half-smoked Balkan Sobranies.

Sullivan went back out to the car, satisfied that Fabrizzio wasn't hiding in the house.

"Grand Central?" the driver asked.

"You guessed it."

*   *   *

At two-thirty A.M., the subway platform was almost deserted.

Almost. Down at one end, standing between two men, was Fabrizzio.

He hadn't yet seen Sullivan approaching from the other end of the platform.

The underground station was dank, dirty, gray, something from an Ohio housewife's nightmare. Steel stanchions, rimed with soot, stood along the platform. The tracks, below, were gummed with trash, which the water dripping from the cracked ceiling and the dirty wind from trains had made into a uniform paper-and-plastic slag. A rat darted under the third rail, indifferent to the lethal wattage of current streaming through it.

"What's going on?" Fabrizzio was asking nervously. "I requested a car to get out of town and you take me here! A train came and we didn't take it!"

"There he is," one of the guards said in a whispered aside to the other.

Fabrizzio turned fearfully to see what the guard had seen. Jack Sullivan moved toward him.

One of the guards shoved him. "Down there." He pointed down a stairway for transit workers that led onto the gravel of the track.

"What!"

The guard pointed a .38 at him. Fabrizzio saw Sullivan coming. He turned and ran down the stairs and into the tunnel.

The guards ran up a stairway behind them.

Sullivan ignored them. He went single-mindedly pursuing Fabrizzio.

Drawing the .44, he ran down onto the tracks.

But he'd brought along something more than the .44. He carried it in a harness under his coat. It made a slight bulge up the middle of his back, but nothing grossly noticeable. It was a sawed-off twelve-gauge shotgun. He'd hacksawed the barrel and the stock off himself, a few days earlier, and kept it waiting in his hotel room. The modified magazine carried eight twelve-gauge shells, and he had eight more stuffed into his pockets, along with an extra clip for the .44. Tucked into his belt were three Ninja shuriken throwing stars. Strapped to his calf, just above his boot, was an AMT .22 backup pistol.

Sullivan knew he was being set up. He had come into this ready to blow the trap apart.

He slowed as he moved further into the darkness. He stopped to listen. He heard the squeak of a rat, and the distant sound of running feet. He moved on.

Fabrizzio was running in blind terror. Thinking: *There is no escape from him.*

As he ran into the darkness, a strange notion came to him.

All the people he had killed were around him in the shadows.

They had always been there. Occasionally, late at night, he slept with the lights on. Because when he turned out the lights, he sometimes saw the faces of the murdered staring at him from the darkest corners of the room, as if from windows into the afterworld. They'd stare out at him and mouth things, speak without making sounds, and he lived in terror of actually hearing what they were saying. That woman he had shot because she had come in and seen him after he had murdered her husband. She'd been nine months pregnant. That old man who had defied the Chicago mob. A harmless old man, but they wanted to make an example. All the others, the dozens of others. . . . Fabrizzio prided himself on feeling nothing about the targets. They were just targets. Or maybe they were like cattle, to be slaughtered for sustenance. Nobody wept for cattle. And in this life there were two kinds of people, the ones who are the cattle and the ones who butcher the cattle. Fabrizzio felt nothing—and yet, in the darkness, sometimes . . .

Sometimes . . .

Like now. He seemed to see faces, hideous faces

staring at him out of the shadows. *The dead, the murdered, coming for him, coming from beyond the grave.*

Fabrizzio screamed as the faces closed in around him. But this time they spoke. "That's him!" one of them said. "Victor said he would have silver hair!"

"He ain't no fuckin' transit worker, you can see that!" another said.

Rough, grimy hands seized Fabrizzio, and he felt himself being dragged off into a side tunnel. There was a little illumination here from ceiling lights at intervals. Normally they were switched on by transit workers when they had to come here to work on the miles of pipes and cables and steam conduits. But the gang had switched them on this time, to light the way into their own private underworld.

There were thirteen of them, and Anvil, their leader, liked it that way. Anvil was a wiry, pallid man. His real name was Johnny Esala. He was Victor's cousin. Like the others, his hair was tousled, matted, crawling with lice; like the others, he wore rags, odds and ends of clothing found in the trash bins. Like the others, his hands and face were masked with filth. Like the others, he was terrified of the upper world, and had lived here, in the tunnels, for three years. Some of the others were a little different. Some of them went up sometimes, to steal things, to get food, to buy drugs. Like Victor, most of the Precious Ones were escapees from asylums who had come here to hide in the miles of tunnels under the stations. There were subway tunnels, utility tunnels, access tunnels, tunnels for water mains. A world of them. A small army of tramps lived there in the winter— and the Precious Ones.

Victor called his gang the Precious Ones because, he said, "We are the jewels the devil has hidden in the earth to keep safe from those who would steal them. In the eyes of the devil, we shine like precious things, because we are his beloved servants."

Victor had a system for contacting his cousin when he needed him—now and then Victor's employers needed something dirty done, something too dirty for a sane man. Nothing was too dirty for Anvil.

"What about the other one?" Anvil's lieutenant, Rat's Kiss, asked.

"He was coming along behind," Anvil explained. "He saw us drag the silver-hair in here. He'll be coming. Victor says kill them both, but kill the big one first. We need the silver-hair alive so the big scarred one will follow.

The gang was armed—they had only two guns, but they had other toys. Knives and other sharp things, things that could be a lot of fun, when they had a victim.

Fabrizzio's heart was pounding and he seemed to hear a roaring in his ears. But his supernatural panic had dissipated. He realized that these men were human. And that he'd been set up to use as bait. He had to make himself think. He had to be calm and watchful, and he would find a way to get away, to survive. . . .

Sullivan slipped into the side tunnel just in time to avoid the train barreling like a thunderbolt down the tracks. It went roaring by, clacking and spitting sparks.

The side tunnel was lit. He chambered a round into the .44 and moved down, looking for any sign of movement up ahead.

A rat scuttled by. Water dripped. That was all.

The ceiling was low, cracked; there were puddles in places where the rainwater had worked through. With the lights and water, he might be electrocuted, if the gang didn't kill him.

Sullivan stopped moving, listening. He heard a shuffle of feet up ahead.

The tunnel forked. To the right it widened into some kind of passage for immense steel pipes. There was just enough room to walk beside the rusted pipes. The voices came from that direction. . . .

"*Come on, mannnn . . .*" they said tauntingly. "*Come and get himmmm!*"

Sullivan saw the flicker of torches to one side of the

right-hand tunnel. They were trying to lure him in there.

He moved to the left-hand tunnel, trotting ahead. The lights were few; the intervals of shadow were long. His skin crawled. This wasn't his kind of fighting environment. Get these bastards into a jungle and he'd have them. . . .

So think of this as a jungle, he told himself. A jungle of tunnels and pipes. What would he do in the jungle? Outflank them.

He kept moving, glancing behind him now and then. Maybe he'd been wrong about the layout of the tunnels. Maybe he'd have to go back.

But up ahead he saw a notch of darkness to the right. He sidled up to it, flattened beside it, and listened. He heard nothing but the plipping of water, echoing from within.

He raised the .44 and stepped around the corner. The passage was narrow and dank. There was a glow of light at the far end; the intervening passage was dark. He moved down the tunnel, crouching to avoid pipes jutting from the ceiling, wondering if he were getting himself lost in a maze.

He reached the end of the connecting passage and paused, heard voices whispering urgently.

"Where is he?"

"I dunno."

"Where is he, Anvil, he shoulda—"

"I said *I don't know!* Now shuddup!"

Sullivan smiled. He'd outflanked them.

He peered around the corner. He was looking down the passage that had forked to the right; the pipes bulked to one side. In the narrow space between concrete wall and pipes, three of the gang were turned away from him. One of them had a rifle in his hands. The others carried what looked like cane-shaped pipes onto which knives had been wired, making them into a sort of scythe.

Sullivan stepped out into the passage, leveled the .44, and said, "Where's Fabrizzio? Tell me and you can go."

The one with the rifle was a redhead with an orange beard so dirty it looked like it had been vomited on his chin. "Shoot him!" the Hispanic behind the redhead shouted. The redhead raised the rifle and fired. The .22 round rang off a pipe and ricocheted down the passage behind Sullivan; the .44 roared in Sullivan's hand, knocking Red off his feet with the impact of its bullet, tearing his chest open so in a moment it was redder than his head.

The others threw themselves down and rolled under the pipes, one of them grabbing the rifle, dragging it with him.

Sullivan knelt and looked under the pipes. There was another passage on the other side.

He didn't like doing it. But he did it anyway: he threw himself down and rolled under. He came up in darkness. The little light came from under the pipes. He saw shapes moving up ahead.

And then a flash, and a bullet struck sparks from a pipe near his head. The narrow passage echoed with the shot.

Sullivan returned fire, pulling the trigger four times. Someone screamed.

He heard running feet. He moved cautiously down the passage, holding himself sideways as he went to make himself harder to hit.

He bumped into something on the floor. Something soft and warm.

He bent, and made out the still form of a member of the gang sprawled facedown, shot through the chest and neck. There was something shiny in his hand. A gun? Sullivan picked it up. Nope, a flashlight.

He carried the flashlight, unlit, in his left hand. The .44 ready in his right, he moved down the passage, feeling his way with his toes, stopping now and then to listen.

He felt a cool, foul breeze on his left cheek. The

darkness was blacker here—a passage opening to the left. Looking at it in the dim light seeping under the pipes, he suspected it had been broken through by the gang. They'd made their own doorway into another tunnel.

He stepped through, tracking the gun to both sides, seeing no one.

This passage was wider. There were pipes overhead, and a light about thirty feet down. Had they come this way? Or had they gone on straight?

He had his answer a second later. There was an insane shriek behind him, and three of them leapt at him from the door he'd just stepped through. The biggest one was a patchy-skinned albino Negro, his eyes an unhealthy shade of blue and his teeth yellow snags. He swung a pipe-scythe at Sullivan's head.

Sullivan ducked; the scythe swished overhead.

And then they were on him, three of them, none as big as he but all of them animal-strong, crazy strong. He felt the .44 torn from his hands. It went skidding down the passage. A knife flashed at his throat. He grabbed the knife hand at the wrist and bent it backward. There was a dry, stick-snapping sound. The subway troll—as Sullivan thought of him—howled and dropped the blade. Another was clinging to Sullivan's right arm, teeth snapping at Sullivan's face like a rabid dog. Sullivan drove an elbow into the troll's ribs and he fell back, gasping.

The albino was trying to get an angle to use the scythe without hurting his friends. Sullivan kicked him in the middle of the chest. He staggered back, slashing at Sullivan's leg with the scythe. The blade ripped through the fabric of Sullivan's fatigues, raked into the meat just above his knee.

Sullivan backed off. The three thugs backed off too, to regroup, one of them crying, holding his broken wrist against his belly. And then Sullivan heard a scraping sound behind him. He turned and saw four more coming from that direction.

Sullivan shrugged.

He reached behind, up into his jacket, took hold of the shortened stock of the shotgun and gave it a twist, unsnapping it from its harness. With practiced ease he pulled it free and swung it up into firing position. He flicked off the safety and squeezed the trigger point-blank. The twelve-guage roared like a small cannon and lit the dim passage with its flash. The lead troll screamed and his face vanished into red pit.

Sullivan spun, at the same time chambering another round, and squeezed off another shot; he held the shotgun down at hip level, propping it on the muscle just beside his hipbone. It kicked viciously, again and again as he fired round after round, filling the air with buzzing clusters of shotgun pellets, shredding everything human they came into contact with. The three who'd first jumped him fell, arms outflung, chunks of their bodies scattered about them in the pool of blood. Sullivan turned to the others—two of them were coming at him, shrieking hatred, faces livid. He pumped the shotgun again . . .

And it jammed.

He swung it by the stock and smashed it into the teeth of the nearest troll; the next one, another albino, threw himself at Sullivan's legs, tackling him. Sullivan pitched over. More Precious Ones came from the door to the left. Sullivan was borne down, smothered in the reeking bodies of madmen.

15
Darkness Within Darkness

When he realized they weren't going to kill him right away, Sullivan gave up struggling. They evidently planned to take him somewhere, and chances were it would be to Fabrizzio.

"How we gonna do it, Anvil, huh?" asked the tallest of the subway trolls. "We gonna feed him to 'em?"

"That's what we gonna do," Anvil said. "Both of 'em."

"Can we play with 'em first?"

"We'll play with 'em. He killed half of us. We'll play with him all right."

This exchange went on as six subway trolls hustled Sullivan along the passage toward the light at the far end. They were clustered around him, one of them pointing the .44 at him, the others with scythes except for one carrying a .32.

They pushed him through a warren of passages; sometimes there was light and sometimes they moved with the aid of the flashlight they'd taken from him. Now and then, the walls would rumble out the message that a subway train was passing nearby.

At last they arrived at a wide chamber, an abandoned subway station several blocks south of Grand Central Station. There were no lights here; a faint illumination came from the far end of the station, which ran at right angles to a newer subway channel, one now in use; the light came from its tracks, faint as starlight.

The old station was shaped like a cylinder cut in half the long way, with concave ceilings adorned with cracked and faded paintings of politicians shaking hands as workers cheerfully dug out the tunnels.

Scores of men had died building these tunnels. It was easy to imagine that their spirits still haunted them, especially when Anvil sent the tall troll to light the crude torches jutting from bulbless lamp cases, the flames making ghostly shadows flicker on the cavelike walls. Rats hurried to be out of the light; a cockroach big as a child's hand scuttled into a drain.

Fabrizzio was there, chained to a stanchion between two sets of tracks, staring in horror at the approaching trolls. Another subway troll guarded Fabrizzio. He was a black man whose face had been horribly scarred by a fire—a lipless, noseless face—the skin resembling a wrinkled paper bag. He slobbered and capered with excitement, seeing them come, his mad eyes glittering in the torchlight.

They went down the utility steps and onto the tracks. The third rail here was dead.

On Anvil's order, the burnt-faced black unlocked Fabrizzio and prodded him down the tracks. In a moment they were standing close beside a pit, which the Precious Ones had dug into the earth between the two sets of tracks. The pit was fifteen feet deep and eight feet wide; it was slightly wider at the bottom than at the top. Anvil shone the flashlight into it. At the bottom were four human skeletons, picked clean; to one of them clung the rags of a transit policeman's uniform. The flashlight glimmered on his badge. On and around the skeletons, running through their ribs, emerging from eye sockets, were rats, dozens of rats, a black-gray-and-pink carpet of living rats, their eyes shining hot pink in the flashlight glare. They chittered and squealed and lifted their greasy, bristly heads to sniff at the air, opening their pink mouths to show sharp yellow incisors.

"Little brothers of the devil," Anvil chanted, "we bring you meat and souls! Give the Precious Ones his protection in return!"

The other Precious Ones returned the litany: "Feed 'em to 'em feed 'em to 'em feed 'em to 'em feed 'em to 'em!"

"As you eat their bodies, eat their souls!"

"Feed 'em to 'em feed 'em to 'em!"

"And as you eat their souls, eat their minds!"

"Feed 'em to 'em feed 'em to 'em!" The group chant rose to a crescendo. The subway trolls gathered around Sullivan and Fabrizzio, urging them to the edge of the pit.

Sullivan shook off the trolls around him and before they could close on him again, he shouted, "Stand back and I'll leap into the damned pit myself. I've always wanted to meet Satan!"

They laughed and cheered and hooted. Anvil said, "Let him meet Satan, then!"

They moved away from him, but ringing him in so he couldn't make a break for it. He moved back from the edge of the pit, then ran for it.

Sprinted straight for it . . .

Reached the edge and leapt, his best broad jump.

He sailed over the pit, was for a moment over the rats, which raised their snouts hungrily for him, and then he came down on the other side. But not quite.

He fell onto the farther edge of the pit, his arms clawing for the rim. He caught it and held on, his legs dangling down inside. Rats leapt for his ankles. Two of them clambered onto him and began crawling up his leg. He shook his leg viciously and they dropped off. He pulled himself up onto the farther side. The trolls howled with disappointment, running around the pit to get at him. The one with the .32 fired; the round kicked up a spray of dirt at his feet.

Sullivan bent and pulled the AMT .22 pistol from beneath his trouser leg, brought it up and fired, punching a small, neat hole in the forehead of the gunman; the subway troll fell forward into the pit, taking the gun with him. The rats squealed and closed over the body. Sullivan fired three more times at the onrushing trolls. The one toting the Automag fell, dropping the gun beside the pit. Two others went down, falling wounded into the pit, screaming with horror as the rats blanketed them, gnawing.

He fired twice more, and the gun was exhausted; three more Precious Ones were still coming at him. He tossed the gun at them and then took two shuriken stars from his belt, one in each hand, and flung them. They were like tiny buzz saws, spinning through the air, embedding themselves in their targets.

The throwing stars sank their points into the throat and forehead of two trolls: the tall one and Anvil. Anvil clutched his throat and fell back, choking, into the pit. "Sataaaaan!" he howled, falling into the embrace of Satan's pets.

The tall one sank to his knees and knelt, staring, a human vegetable. But the troll with the burned face was upon Sullivan, his distorted features misshapen even further wth kill-lust, his long, filth-blackened nails clawing at the Specialist's eyes.

Sullivan grabbed the madman's wrists in his two hands and wrestled him backward toward the edge of the pit. The madman was strong, insanely strong, and for a moment they tottered, both of them about to fall.

All the time, Sullivan was thinking: Where's Fabrizzio?

Fabrizzio had used the distraction Sullivan caused to run for the transverse subway tracks, trying desperately to get back to the world of electric lights and sanity.

Sullivan teetered on the edge of the pit, felt the dirt rim crumble under his left foot as the madman tried to force him over.

The Specialist had had enough. He let go of the madman's wrists and jumped back, then turned his back to the pit. The troll circled and came at him, trying to drive him in. Sullivan took the madman by the forearm and judo-flipped him over his hip, into the rat pit.

Scooping up the .44, Sullivan turned and ran after Fabrizzio.

Fabrizzio sprinted to the end of the unused tracks and through the archlike opening that led onto the other set of tracks.

A rumbling sound grew, swelled in the walls.

Sullivan shouted, "You can run, you bastard, but you can't hide," as he pounded down the tracks, reached the arches, ran through to the right.

Fabrizzio was thirty feet ahead. Sullivan raised the Automag—and then lowered it. Killing Fabrizzio that way would be too easy. He wanted him in his hands. He holstered the gun and increased his speed. The rumble behind him increased its volume . . .

Fabrizzio looked over his shoulder. Seeing Sullivan, his eyes widened. He realized he wasn't going to escape by running. He turned and looked desperately around. He found a broken bottle on the tracks, picked it up, and ran at Sullivan with it, panting with fear and hate, sweat pasting his silvery hair to his head.

Sullivan stood there, waiting for him.

Behind Sullivan, the train rumbled nearer.

Fabrizzio came within reach, and slashed at Sullivan's belly with the bottle's broken edge. Sullivan sucked his gut in, and the broken glass slashed harmlessly by, an eighth of an inch from his skin. As Fabrizzio's arm flashed by, Sullivan grabbed it at the wrist and twisted.

Fabrizzio grunted with pain, dropping the bottle. He punched at Sullivan's throat but Sullivan had ducked his head, taking the punch on his jaw, grunting with the impact. With his free hand he caught Fabrizzio's fist, and he wrenched it around behind Fabrizzio's back, then gave it a half-turn in a way it wasn't meant to turn. Fabrizzio screamed with pain as his arm dislocated.

Sullivan kicked Fabrizzio over onto his face. The assassin lay sobbing on the tracks.

Sullivan turned, hearing a horn blast behind him. A

subway train was bearing down on him, the engineer looking at him with horror, hitting the brakes—but too late. Sullivan leapt across the tracks, landing atop the insulation over the third rail, and bounced from that through the arches into the abandoned tunnel.

He heard Fabrizzio scream behind him.

Sullivan got up, turned, and watched the subway train grind by. It slowed to a stop in the tunnel. The engineer was calling headquarters to ask what he should do, because he thought he had just run a guy down. . . .

Sullivan went back to the other set of subway tracks and walked along beside the train till he found the proof he was looking for: Fabrizzio's severed head, grinning bloodily up at him from between two train wheels.

Sullivan turned away, and walked back down the tracks. He walked a quarter of a mile, to a subway station. People waiting on the platform stared at him as he emerged from the tunnel. He walked up the steps onto the platform, noting the location of the station. He walked up to the street and hailed a cab.

There was a great deal more he had to do.

16

Two Kinds of Hell

There were machines to either side of her. The machines were listening to her heart, and to the electric pulses of her brain. Wires ran from the machines to conductors pasted to her chest, her forehead.

Bonnie was asleep, a sheet drawn up to her neck. There was a bandage on the back of her neck and another around her throat.

"She's no longer on the critical list," the young intern told Sullivan, looking at the clipboard. "She's definitely recovering. She had been on a respirator for the first thirty-six hours—the shrapnel had partly paralyzed her, and her lungs weren't getting their operating signals. But the paralysis passed after the operation. She was lucky. If the shrapnel had penetrated another tenth of a centimeter, she'd have been paralyzed for life."

"But . . . she's going to be all right?" Sullivan asked.

The intern nodded, winked, and left the room. Across from Bonnie, an old woman lay staring at the ceiling. She had shrunk to a wisp of a woman, and was reduced to replaying sad memories.

Sullivan looked back at Bonnie—and saw her smiling at him.

"Hi, Jack," she said. Her voice was a little raspy, but strong.

"Hi." He went to her bedside and took her hand. "How you feel?"

"Rocky. But I can feel myself, even the discomfort, and I guess that's lucky, from what they tell me."

He nodded. "They say you're going to be okay." He took a deep breath. "I'm sorry. I shouldn't have stayed on with you when I knew there was a contract on me."

She said, "Hey, I take it as flattery."

"For what it's worth, the guy won't be firing any more grenades at anyone."

"I guess that's good. . . . But what now, Jack?"

"Legion left the country. He's in Sicily. I'll be going after him."

She sighed. "I don't know . . ."

"I do. I know what I have to do. You want me to bring you anything?"

"Maybe newspapers, magazines."

"Okay, I'll be right back. I'll go get them at the gift shop downstairs."

He went out into the hall, down past the nurse's station to the elevators. In the gift shop he bought four magazines, a box of candy, and a bouquet of carnations. He rode the elevator up with two doctors who were talking about colonoscopies in excessive detail, and walked back to her room.

The door was closed now. He opened it and a large, hairy male nurse in a starched white uniform blocked his way. "Can't come in. She can't see anybody right now," the guy said sullenly.

"I just want to give her these magazines," Sullivan said. "And the flowers."

"I'll give to her. She can't see anyone."

There were muffled sounds of protest coming from the room behind the male nurse. "She's taking her medicine," the nurse said.

Sullivan didn't like the way the guy smiled as he said it.

And then he heard the old woman across from Bonnie say, "What's going on, what are you doing to her?"

The nurse turned to look over his shoulder. "Shuddup, lady!"

Sullivan dropped the magazines, candy, and flowers and slammed his shoulder into the half-open door, knocking the door's edge into the "nurse." The impostor staggered back. Sullivan stepped in and kicked the guy hard in the gut. He folded up, bending forward sharply at the waist, his jaw running into Sullivan's fist on the way up. He spun and fell senseless.

Another phony male nurse at the bed was pressing a pillow over Bonnie's face, trying to smother her.

Seeing Sullivan move toward him, he let go of the pillow and tugged a small silver pistol from his tunic pocket. Sullivan drew the .44, but not quite quick enough. The guy had his gun leveled first.

Bonnie pushed the pillow away and knocked the gunman's pistol up. The gun fired into the ceiling. Sullivan trained the .44 and shot the thug dead-center through the heart. Blood splashed onto Bonnie's white bedsheet. The old woman screamed. The hardman fell.

Sullivan holstered the Automag.

He went to Bonnie, touching her face tenderly. "You okay, Bonnie?"

"Yeah. I think so."

Nurses rushed in, demanding an explanation.

Sullivan glanced at his watch. It was ten-thirty A.M. He went to the phone by the bed and called Sanson. The secretary at the FBI put him on the line almost immediately.

"Sullivan?"

"Yeah. I need a favor. Part of the deal for the commando unit. I need you to call your contacts in NYPD, set up police protection for Bonnie Roland in room 1516 at New York Hospital. And I'll need you to make some explanations for me, cover for me. I just had to shoot a guy here."

"Christ, Sullivan!"

"Couldn't help it. He was trying to smother Bonnie, and when he blew that he tried to shoot us both. I figure Crackwell sent him. There's another one here still alive."

"Okay. I'll see what I can do. You got that phony I.D. of yours around?"

"Yeah."

"You'll need it. I'll see if I can head off the cops so you don't have to make a statement."

"Thanks." He hung up. As security cops and doctors and nurses crowded around, asking questions, Sullivan pushed through them to the hall, picked up the flowers, magazines, and candy. He rearranged the flowers, then brought them to her and calmly put them in the vase.

An orderly hauled the corpse from the room.

Crackwell hadn't heard from Fabrizzio or Sullivan, so he figured Victor's sick pets under Grand Central had taken care of them both. It was eleven A.M. He sat in Legion's office drinking coffee, waiting for a report from the two he had sent to take care of the girl in the hospital.

He heard the doorbell ring. He frowned. He wasn't expecting anyone. But maybe it was a telegram from the boss.

Then he heard a shout, and a big thump. Two more thumps and a crash, and then a cry of pain. Footsteps came down the hall.

Crackwell fumbled in the desk for a gun. He found a pistol, broke it open, and saw it was unloaded.

And then the door opened.

Crackwell looked up. His mouth went dry. His heart began to bang in his chest. Sweat broke out on his palms.

The Speicalist stood in the doorway. He had one of the bodyguards by the throat and was dragging him into the room. The man was out cold. Sullivan lifted him up and tossed him onto the desk.

Crackwell leapt up, overturning his chair, and stared down at the unconscious man sprawled over the desk.

Sullivan stepped to the right of the door, just as the

other bodyguard ran up behind him. The man ran into the room, and Sullivan simply stretched a leg out and tripped him. The second bodyguard fell heavily onto the floor, skidding a few feet, the gun spinning from his hand.

Sullivan had a .44 Automag in his hand. He gave Crackwell a wintry smile.

"You shouldn't have done it, Crackwell. You shouldn't have sent them after her."

The second bodyguard was getting groggily to his feet. Sullivan kicked him cleanly, and he fell down again. The kick had been casual, as a boy will kick a can as he's walking down the street.

"I don't know what you're—" Crackwell began.

Sullivan snarled and bent over, grabbed the underside of the desk and flipped the whole thing over, sending papers and the phone flying, flopping the unconscious bodyguard to the floor. Crackwell had to jump back to keep the desk from falling on his feet.

The second bodyguard tried to get up again, managed to get halfway to his feet—Sullivan whacked him across the head with the barrel of the .44 and he fell like a flour sack.

Sullivan came around the desk and grabbed Crackwell by the shirt front, twisting it in his hand, jerking him closer; he thrust the tip of the gun barrle into one of Crackwell's ears.

"You hear what happened to Carlos Ajidas?" Sullivan asked with deadly softness.

"Uh—yeah, I heard."

"You heard what happened to the Gonzales brothers?"

"Yeah, yeah, sure—"

"How about those assholes in the ski masks you and Legion sent to rough up Bonnie Roland? You know what happened to them?"

"Sure, sure, I know—"

"Then why are you trying to lie to me? Carlos Ajidas tried to lie to me. I blew his brains out. You know where Fabrizzio is? He's chopped and diced in a tunnel near Grand Central Station. You know where those punks are you tried to trap me with? Huh?"

"Uh—no!"

"Good. I'll have the pleasure of showing you. Come on!"

He shoved Crackwell toward the door. They stepped over the unconscious men and went down the hall to the front door, Crackwell looking nervously over his shoulder at the gun. Sullivan said, "Hold it right here," just before they reached the door. He frisked Crackwell, then holstered his own gun. "Okay, you want to see how good a quick-draw artist I am, just try to fuck with me on the way. Now, go on, out to the car."

Sullivan had rented a light blue dodge Charger. "You're driving," Sullivan told him.

Crackwell got in behind the wheel. Sullivan climbed in beside him and tossed him the keys. "We're going to Thirty-third and Park Avenue," Sullivan said.

"Look," Crackwell said, licking his lips, "whatever you've got in mind—it's unnecessary. Everything I've done has been under orders. Legion is the man you want. He—"

"Shut up and drive."

"I know what you're thinking," Sullivan said as he and Crackwell walked down into the subway station. "You're thinking there'll be people on the subway platform, maybe even a cop. You're thinking of yelling for help. But I'm already wanted by the cops, Crackwell. I've got nothing to lose by shooting you in front of them." This wasn't strictly true, but Crackwell didn't know that. "You say a word, Crackwell, I'll drill you right there."

"Look, we can work out a deal—"

"Shut up."

Sullivan was carrying a coil of rope over one arm. In his coat was a pocket-sized cassette recorder. He carried a flashlight in his left hand.

Sullivan had the subway tokens. They went through the turnstiles and down onto the platform.

"Down onto the tracks," Sullivan whispered. "There's steps over there."

"Are you crazy?"

Sullivan put his hand into his coat, onto the gun butt. Crackwell went down the steps.

Sullivan followed. People stared but said nothing.

"To the left," Sullivan said. They walked down the tunnel, Crackwell going ahead. When they'd come to the edge of the deeper tunnel darkness, Crackwell turned and said, "I'm not going. You're going to tie me to the tracks. Like you did Fabrizzio."

"No, that's not what I'm going to do."

"I don't believe you."

Sullivan drew the gun. "The truth is, I'm not going to kill you at all, unless you make me. It's all up to you."

Crackwell swallowed, and looked at the gun. He turned and plodded deeper into the darkness.

After a while they felt a vibration through the tracks. Rats scurried to get out of the way of the oncoming train.

Seeing the rats, Crackwell recoiled, gasping, biting his finger.

"You're scared of rats?" Sullivan asked.

Crackwell nodded, his eyes wide.

"A phobia?" Sullivan asked.

Crackwell nodded again.

"Good," Sullivan said.

The train was thundering down on them, its headlights shining like the eyes of a dragon in its cave.

"What'll we do!" Crackwell yelled. "It's gonna run us down!"

Sullivan took him by the arm and led him over the third rail, through the arches into the abandoned subway station. The torches had gone out. Sullivan turned on the flashlight and shoved Crackwell down the tracks. The train roared behind them, its lights flickering through the archways. Rats scrambled away from their grisly work on the corpses Sullivan had left at the edge of the pit.

Crackwell gagged, and tried to turn away, covering his eyes.

Sullivan tied the rope around Crackwell's chest, looped it under his armpits, threw the other end over a beam above the pit.

"What . . . what are you doing?" Crackwell asked, his voice quavering.

Humming, Sullivan walked him over to the pit. He held one end of the rope firmly—and shoved Crackwell into the rat pit.

Crackwell screamed, falling backward into the hell within hell, the darkness within darkness.

Sullivan pulled the rope taut, and Crackwell jerked to a stop, a few feet above the swarm of rodents in the rat pit. Holding the line wrapped around his arm with one hand, with the other Sullivan shone the light down into the pit.

Crackwell burst into sobs, pleading, when he saw the dozens of pairs of red eyes, the sinuous rodent bodies, the rasping pink tails, the wriggling snouts and sharp incisors. He gagged at the stench, vomited when he saw the chewed-over remains of the gang in the pit, with rats nosing into entrails.

"Let me out, Sullivan, for God's sake let me out!" he howled, trying to claw his way up the rope. But his efforts only made him slip a little farther down. The rats jumped up to nip at his heels. He screamed again.

"You sing to the Feds about the dope operation, Crackwell, I'll let you go! You'll go to jail but it'll be better than getting fed to our little friends down there."

"Anything! I'll do anything! I'll tell them everything I know!"

"You know what, Crackwell? I don't believe you. You're just saying it. You don't really mean it. You figure as soon as you get out, I'll let you go, and you can maybe leave town. You won't have to sing."

"No, no! I swear to you!"

"I don't believe it. What good is your word? Yeah, I guess I'll feed you to them."

He lowered Crackwell a little more. The rats leapt, and some of them clutched Crackwell's ankles, beginning to climb onto him. He screamed and kicked them away. "Please! Please, anything!"

"You know, I do believe those creeps who kept these little guys here must have trained them," Sullivan said musingly. "They're much more aggressive than rats usually are. I'll bet if I leave you hanging there, they'll keep jumping at you till they finally swarm over you. Might take a few hours—"

"For God's sake, this is sadistic!"

"Sadistic? How about sending thugs to kill a woman in her hospital bed, Crackwell? Or to tie her to a chair and beat her with lead pipes, hm?"

"That was Legion's idea!"

"You were part of it, Crackwell. You implemented all of it. Don't talk to me about cruelty. You, the heroin pusher, knowing what it does to people. You, the guy who sends punks to beat up old men."

"I'm sorry! I was wrong! Please! I can't stand it! I'm going mad!"

"Maybe I'll truss you up differently—so your dick is dangling down—"

"NOOOOO!"

Crackwell screamed for a while, then broke into babbling.

When the babbling had quieted a little, Sullivan said, "You hear me Crackwell?"

"Please please please please—"

"You'll do what I tell you?"

"Yes yes yes yes yes—"

"You know that I'll find you if you fail me. I'll bring you back here again. They'll be here waiting for you."

"No no no no!"

Sullivan pulled on the rope, hauling Crackwell up out of the pit. He reached over and dragged him into the dirt. He fell sobbing at Sullivan's feet, clutching Sullivan's ankles. "I'll do anything, anything, I'm your servant, just don't, don't, don't . . ."

"Now you've got the right attitude. Come on." He grabbed the rope and used it like a leash to yank Crackwell out of the tunnel and up into the light of day.

Crackwell sat in Sanson's office, talking into the tape recorder. He was staring at the wall, his eyes wide. His hands were clutching his knees, his knuckles white. He named names, giving a detailed report of Legion's dope-dealing connections. When he was through, they switched off the tape recorder and he signed a confession. His court-appointed attorney, an idealistic young man barely old enough to shave, several times tried to object. But it was Crackwell himself, turning to the lawyer urgently, who said, "Please! No one coerced me into this confession! I . . . I want to make it! I must!"

The lawyer looked sharply at Sullivan. "What did you do to scare him into this?"

True to Sullivan's instructions, Crackwell went on, "No, no! He didn't scare me! No one did! I just . . . just realized it was wrong!"

The lawyer, disgusted, gave up and left. After a while, Sanson's assistants came to take Crackwell away. Crackwell turned to Sullivan and whispered, "Did I do right? You won't take me back . . . back there?"

"You don't have to go back there ever, so long as you go through with the court follow-up," Sullivan said.

Crackwell nodded eagerly, too many times, his eyes glassy. Hands shaking, ghost-pale, he allowed himself to be led out.

Sullivan had been taking notes. He looked over his two pages of notebook scribblings, and nodded. He tore it off the notebook, folded it, and put it into his coat pocket.

He stood up, nodded at Sanson, and turned to go.

"Hold it," Sanson said. Sullivan looked at him

quizzically. Sanson went on, "Off the record—what did you do to him?"

"Showed him a little preview of hell," Sullivan said. "He got religion, fast."

Sanson shrugged. "Listen—leave Legion to us, Sullivan."

Sullivan shook his head. "No can do. You've got enough, with Krinsky and Crackwell, to put all Legion's associates away, and to trace their overseas connections. Legion is mine now. He put Bonnie in the hospital. Through his intermediary—but he's responsible. Maybe you think it's unprofessional to personalize the kind of work I do. But Legion made it personal when he hit Bonnie. He's had a lot of people killed—you know that as well as I do. He deserves what I'm going to give him. After this . . ." Sullivan smiled. "I'll try to keep personal vengeance out of it."

"Yeah. Sure. Get out of here. I don't know what you're going to do, never heard of any of it."

Sullivan nodded and walked out.

In the hall he looked at his watch. He had just time enough to make his plane.

17

The Sicilian Connection

After the perpetually overcast skies of New York on the verge of winter, the sunshine glare of Palermo was startling. Sullivan put on his sunglasses and walked off the plane to the bus that would take them to the airport's main building.

He showed the customs officials his false passport, in the name Richard Stark, answered the usual questions about his plans with the bland skill of the frequent traveler, and carried his bag out to the front of the building. A line of cabs waited out front, the cabdrivers calling out the window, "Hey, American, very fine taxi tour!"

Sullivan knew that was a memorized line and that most of them couldn't speak English. He walked down the line saying, "I need someone who can speak English."

The fourth one down said, "*Si,* I speak English *molto bene!*"

Sullivan got in, and they drove down the beach road toward downtown Palermo. "I know very good hotel," the driver said. He was a jolly-faced man with gray hair and a bushy mustache. He swayed a little to the music coming over the radio.

"What's your name?" Sullivan asked.

"Alfredo Baroni."

"Alfredo, take me to the Hotel Pasolini. Directly."

"Sure, anything you say, that's what Alfredo do. One time, I live New York City, you ever been there?" Without pausing for an answer, he launched into a harangue about his erstwhile life in New York. Sullivan said "Uh-huh" now and then, and looked out the window at the rocky coastline. Here and there were summer houses, closed and shuttered, looking desolate. The land was parched and brown, mostly flat in this area; hills rose steel blue in the distance.

They passed through Palermo, a city of sun-washed clay-colored buildings, squared off and red-tiled in the Mediterranean manner; there was a Baroque cathedral and ornately gated cemeteries said to contain entrances to catacombs.

"Alfredo," Sullivan said after a while, "how would you like to earn some extra money? Silly question. So tell me—you know Sicily?"

Alfredo laughed. "Does a man know his wife's breasts! *Si!*"

"Good. I'm looking for the house of the family Montevori. You know where it is?"

"Sure, is a big, beautiful house, south Palermo! You want to take pictures?"

"Not exactly." Legion was staying at the Montevoris' mansion.

Alfredo looked at Sullivan in the rearview mirror, a little suspiciously. "What you want to do? You know Signor Montevori? You go for visit?"

"Not exactly that either. What time is it here?"

"What time? Sicilian time, two o'clock."

"Okay. You meet me at the front of my hotel at ten o'clock tonight, you'll earn some money."

"Alfredo will be there."

They pulled up at the Hotel Pasolini. Sullivan paid, tipped extravagantly, and got out.

It was a modern hotel, built by a West German hotel chain. It was imitatively modern, with garish angles and sweeping panes of glass. It reminded Sullivan of the modern-style churches that were springing up around

America, with their stylized steeples and cartoon simplifications of traditional stained-glass figures. In short, it was ugly.

Sullivan sighed and carried his bag in past plastic potted plants and a badly designed water fountain.

But he had a reason for selecting this hotel. He'd called Ollie Tryst, now a married man in Louisiana, for advice about where to find ordnance in Palermo. Sullivan had come without guns—if he'd traveled with his usual armament the metal detector in the airport would have gone mad with the alarms. Ollie had said this hotel's groundskeeper sometimes sold black-market guns on the side, and somehow he was suspicious if the buyer didn't stay at his hotel.

Sullivan walked through an enormous, echoing lobby that gave him a chill like an empty theater at night; he registered and asked that a menu be sent to his room. He was informed that at this hour luncheon was no longer served, and Sullivan remembered that Europeans are neurotically strict about when they eat.

He managed to get them to send up an antipasto and some melon, and he went to his room. It was more or less like a room in any Holiday Inn, but it was four times the price.

He sat on the balcony, four stories up. The hotel was on the seaward edge of town. Terraced grounds stretched out to an olive orchard. The beach was about a mile away, but small hotel buses took the guests there every morning. He could just make out a cobalt-blue swatch of sea. A brisk wind off the sea whipped the palm trees the hotel had planted around its white-concrete walks.

The antipasto and melon arrived, and Sullivan ate greedily. He drank thick black Sicilian coffee, and watched the grounds below. He was looking for the groundskeeper. Tryst had said his name was Pincello.

Sullivan felt naked without a gun. Naked—and vulnerable. Legion could have had the airports watched. They could have seen him come in, could now be on their way to execute him.

Sullivan knew that Legion's Sicilian associates were almost certainly Cosa Nostra. Legion was not a Mafia initiate, but he had business contacts with them, and they would be quite willing to protect their contacts. One out of three Sicilians worked in some way with the Cosa Nostra. And the rest of the people were related to the people who worked for it. Not even the Specialist could hope to fight an army that big alone. He had to get in, get Legion, do the job, and get out *fast*.

A man with a cigarette in his mouth pushed a wheelbarrow along one of the landscaped terraces, trailing smoke. Sullivan watched him for a few minutes, then went downstairs and out onto the grounds. He walked out to the terrace, trying to be careful about where he stepped.

The man with the wheelbarrow wore overalls and a patchy blue sweatshirt, its sleeves rolled up. There was a crude tattoo of the Madonna on his tanned, veined forearm. The cigarette dangled from his lips as he worked; he squinted against its smoke. He was a middle-aged man with a gray mustache, thinning gray hair, a low forehead, and a sour expression.

Sullivan said "Pincello?".

The man straightened and said something in Italian, which Sullivan took to mean: *Who the hell are you?*

"My name's Stark," Sullivan said. "Oliver Tryst sent me. You speak any English?"

"What you want?"

"Guns," Sullivan said simply.

"You don't come here talk for that. The shed. Toolshed, over there, other side, sunset!" Irritably, as if any fool should know that.

"I'll be there," Sullivan said. "I'll need—"

"We don't talk about it now. Very bad, I'm seen talking here."

"I need it tonight," Sullivan said.

"You crazy, eh?"

"Tonight," Sullivan said. "I'll pay well. I need a submachine gun, a good silenced pistol, a Beretta would do, ammo. Grenades, if you have them. A sniper's rifle."

"What you do, start an army? You Communist?"

"Not hardly."

"Too bad. I am. But I bring you what I can. Best can do. You bring American dollars. Not lire. Get hell out of here now."

Sullivan walked away.

"Hey, be careful, you step my flowers, damn you!" Pincello called after him.

At sunset, Sullivan found the toolshed set up near a blank back wall of the hotel. The toolshed was old and rustic, contrasting strangely with the hotel's looming modernity. It was cold this time of year in the evening, and the wind had taken on an icy edge. A small plume of smoke rose from the toolshed. Beyond it, the sky was smashed with scarlet and lurid orange. The vicious Mediterranean mosquitoes dive-bombed Sullivan's face. He slashed irritably at them, and knocked on the door of the shed.

Pincello opened the door and glared out at him as if he'd never seen him before.

"I brought the money," Sullivan said.

He'd said the magic words. Pincello opened the door.

It was close and musty inside. A kerosene lamp gave the wooden interior a yellow basting. To the left were stacks of garden tools, their blades crusted with dried dirt. The dirt the Romans, the Greeks, the Germans, and other conquerors had trod. To the right were a potbellied wood-burning stove and a ratty couch. Nothing else, except a bottle of red wine in an unlabeled blue bottle on a crude wooden table beside the couch, and two smudged glasses. Pincello closed the door behind Sullivan. "You want drink?"

Surprised by the hospitality, Sullivan said, "Thanks," accepting a glass of wine.

They drank it off. The wine was good but tasted as if it had been aged all of two days.

Pincello clapped down the glass. The formalities done, he put out his hand, palm up. "One thousand dollars," he said.

"Depends on what you've got," Sullivan said. "For that price, you'd better have an Exocet missile for me."

"Price is not for guns, it is for risk. What you do here, you do without permission. I know that. I look at you, I know."

By "without permission," he meant without the Mafia's permission.

"They find out," Pincello went on, "they kill me, my wife, my children, my uncles, my aunts, my in-laws, my dogs and my cats. They even pull up my flowers, you know? One thousand dollars, no haggle."

Sullivan nodded. "Okay."

He took out his billfold, counted out five one-hundred-dollar bills and ten fifties, nearly emptying the billfold. But he had credit cards—in the name Richard Stark—and traveler's checks.

He gave Pinchello the cash. "American money," Pinchello said appreciatively, counting. "That's good. I keep it for a while, it goes up against the lira. Worth more, you know?"

He tucked it into a pocket and went to the stack of tools. He moved an armful of hoes away, leaned them on another wall, returned to the place they'd stood, and removed four floorboards. He reached into the space under the boards and pulled out a metal box. It was one of the standard methods for hiding guns. Sullivan used it himself.

He opened the box and spread an oilcloth, displaying four guns. There was a Thompson submachine gun, looking like something from a forties gangster movie, a Beretta 93, an Italian Army submachine gun, and a Browning target rifle, .28, with a detachable stock. There was a silencer for the Beretta.

Sullivan looked the weapons over critically. They were scratched and spotted with rust, but they'd been recently oiled and they seemed clean. "You can keep the

Italian SMG," Sullivan said. "It's not reliable. I'll take the others, if you've got ammo for them, and if they test out."

"Test? You want to test?"

"Not here, of course, but you don't expect me to buy weapons and risk my ass using them without testing them, do you?"

Pincello shrugged. "Okay. I loan you my truck, you take them to the beach. Test them the beach below the cliffs. Anybody catches you, you say you stole the truck, eh?"

"You got it. You know, if the guns don't test out, there's no way you're going to keep that money and live."

Sullivan said it casually. Pincello, equally casual, nodded that he understood.

Sullivan took the guns in a canvas duffel bag, padded out with spare clothing. He found a secluded beach and, in the afterglow of sunset, tested the weapons. The Thompson jerked to the left and it made a hell of a noise, but it seemed to work all right. He had to reset the sights on the rifle. The Beretta stood up. It was a sale. He returned the truck, picked up an extra box of ammo, camouflaged it in the duffel, and went to wait for Alfredo.

Alfredo showed up at ten-thirty. Sullivan got in the cab, carrying the duffel bag containing the rifle, the Thompson, and the pile of clothing. The Beretta was in his pocket. It was loaded with a ten-round magazine.

Alfredo looked nervously at the duffel but said nothing. Sullivan said, "The Montevori house. Servants' entrance."

Alfredo raised an eyebrow. His earlier jolliness was gone. "What you do there?"

"I'm a photographer, taking pictures of the house. They have a special architecture. I tried to get permission, they said no. I do it anyway. No one gets hurt from a photo, eh?"

"That's a big camera you got," Alfredo said, looking over his shoulder at the duffel.

"Got a lot of cameras. For different kinds of shots." He took out a roll of lira notes equivalent to a hundred American dollars and passed it to Alfredo. Alfredo took it, counted it, looked impressed, and started the car.

The Montevori house was in the old section of Palermo. Most of the old houses here were snugged together, their brightly painted porchless doors opening directly onto the cobbled streets, without sidewalk. Someone emptied dishwater out a window as they passed, narrowly missing the cab.

The Montevori house was on a small hill, set apart from the others by a narrow street that ran all the way around it, and a vine-covered wall cracked with age, showing bricks through the plaster in places.

Sullivan ordered Alfredo to circle the house twice as he looked it over. The wall was about ten feet high. There was a black metal gate, locked, at the front, and a green-painted wooden door in the wall provided a side entrance.

Sullivan looked at Alfredo and wondered what he'd do if he heard gunshots. Would he wait? Probably not. So he might have to go it on foot.

It was a big house. There would be a good number of people in it, probably a family, innocent bystanders. He couldn't kill them. If one of them saw him, they'd describe him not only to the local cops but also to the Sicilian Mafia's enforcers. He'd never get out through the airport. It would have to be by stolen boat.

He'd have to do his best.

"Alfredo, how about if you rent me this car?"

"Leave you with it? No, please, very sorry. No, no—"

"All right. Pull up by this door. Wait here for me. You wait, I'll give you three times as much money when I get out."

Alfredo nodded, but said nothing. He seemed sullen. Sullivan didn't like that.

The cab pulled up and Sullivan got out, carrying the

duffel bag. He walked around the corner to the back wall of the house.

There were a few streetlamps and no moon. The street was shadowy. A little yellow light spilled over the wall from the upper reaches of the Montevori house. It was a villa, three stories, each story set a little back from the one preceding it, making three consecutive expanses of red tiled roof. On the second story was a terrace, with a roof around it. No one on the terrace.

Sullivan wondered if he'd come with too much firepower. He might not need the Thompson and the Browning. He laid the duffel on the sidewalk and looked around.

The street was deserted. Farther down the hill two teenagers on a Vespa motor scooter rode by, and were gone from sight.

Sullivan backed up from the wall, took a running leap, and grabbed at the upper edge. He missed, and fell back. He tried again; this time he made it. He clung there a moment, then did a pull-up, elbow-crawled onto the wall, and looked over into the back garden. There were rosebushes, their roses dying, brightly colored flowerpots set to either side of red-brick walks, and a small grove of fig trees. A man sat under the fig trees, smoking a cigarette, staring critically at his shoes. He was sitting on a white, ornate metal bench. There was a shotgun across his lap. One sentry in the back. The place looked sedate, smug in homey security. The Montevoris had probably never been attacked at home. They were overconfident.

Sullivan dropped to the sidewalk, deciding he wouldn't need the heavy equipment at this point. He hid the duffel bag in an alley trashcan, and then returned to the wall, climbing over it on the rear corner, behind the sentry. He dropped silently into the mulch of the garden. The sentry yawned and stretched. Sullivan drew his gun and screwed the silencer onto it. He crept up behind the sentry and pointed the gun at the back of his head.

But then he saw that the sentry was a young man, in his early twenties. He was not necessarily a Mafia killer. Working for the local godfather in Sicily was as common as getting a summer job at McDonald's in the states. He'd probably never had to shoot anyone. Sullivan couldn't shoot in him in the back of the head.

Instead, he hit him hard, but not too hard, with the gun barrel. He did it expertly. The young sentry fell over. Sullivan propped him back in the chair, making it look as if he were dozing. Then he moved toward the house.

Legion and Ennio Montevori were playing cards in the dining room with Ennio's brother Marcello when the maid came in, Alfredo Baroni behind her, hat in hand.

"Excuse me, Signor Montevori," he said humbly, in Italian. "I have something to tell you. My conscience tells me I must. A man is coming into your house, and I think he has guns."

Montevori was a big-bellied man with a few strands of gray hair plastered over his bald head. He wore wire-rim glasses, suit pants, a blue shirt with the sleeves rolled up, and suspenders. He stood abruptly and said, "What is this you say? How do you know this?"

Alfredo shuffled his feet and worried his hat in his fingers. "This man hired me to drive him, Signor Montevori. Then he came here and asked me to wait. He said he wanted to take pictures. But to look at the man . . ."

As Alfredo explained, Legion looked back and forth between them, their sense of urgency infecting him, though he didn't understand a word of Italian.

"An American, you say," Montevori said musingly. He spoke to Legion in English: "He says a man from America, a big man with a scar on his face, is somewhere on the grounds, perhaps with a gun—"

"Sullivan!" Legion burst out, leaping to his feet. He looked desperately around. "You must hide me! The bastard wants to murder me! He is a killer! How could he have followed me? He must have killed Fabrizzio. It must be true what they say about him—"

Montevori shouted for his bodyguards. Then he turned to Legion. "And what do they say?"

"He's supposed to be the most dangerous man in the United States. They call him the Specialist."

Coretti and Albano came in. "What is it you need, Signor Montevori?" Albano asked in Italian.

"Where is your brother?"

"He was watching out back, *signor*."

"You'd better check on him, and everywhere else. Call Calioto for some help. There's a man on the grounds— the man called the Specialist. Some kind of American assassin."

Coretti's eyes had narrowed. He was a lean, ferret-faced man with slicked-back black hair. "The Specialist? This man killed my Uncle Vince in France! Where is he?" He drew his gun and stalked around the room, opening doors, making a great show of looking angrily for the Specialist. There were four doors in the dining room, one in each wall. When he opened the third, he stepped back gasping, his bravado gone. A man of terrifying aspect stood in the door. Tall, broad-chested, grim-eyed, scar-faced, a gun in his hand held so casually and yet with such control it could have been an organic part of him.

Coretti turned to run, and then remembered that the others were watching, and he was armed. He forced himself to face the Specialist, firing the gun wildly.

Coretti's shot missed by a good six inches. Sullivan cut him down with a single round to the forehead, then stepped to one side of the door as Albano opened up with a revolver. Two rounds buried themselves in the wall beside Sullivan, the detonations ringing off the high ceiling.

Sullivan was wishing he'd brought the Thompson after all.

Sullivan opened up on Albano, shot him twice in the chest, and before he'd hit the floor he was tracking the gun to find Legion.

But Legion had run from the room, Montevori and his cousin close behind him.

Sullivan had strong evidence that Montevori was part of Legion's dope-smuggling operation, and he was a known member of the Cosa Nostra; both facts made him fair game as far as Sullivan was concerned. If he got in the way, he'd get what was coming to Legion.

Sullivan, crossing the room to follow Legion through the opposite door, saw Alfredo running out the front way. Sullivan guessed what had happened. He had underestimated the close-knittedness of Sicilians.

Sullivan's bootsteps echoed in the halls as he ran after Legion, Montevori, and his cousin. The three men had run out a side door into the driveway beside the house. Sullivan ran through the door in time to see a car backing out, a servant throwing wide the gates for it.

Sullivan ran to catch up, raising the Beretta to fire through the windshield of the car. But the slugs skipped off the bullet-resistant glass. And then the gardener charged Sullivan, a big man with a bushy beard and bared teeth, raising a weed-cutting scythe over his head as he came.

Sullivan couldn't just shoot him down. He was simply loyal to his employer, was not a professional thug like Coretti, and probably had a family. It was part of Sullivan's lifework to make judgments of that kind in the split seconds he had in which to make decisions. He leapt back. The scythe whined past his head, missing by an inch. Sullivan smashed his gun butt into the man's elbow. The gardener howled and dropped the scythe. Sullivan kicked him in the gut, and then bowled him over. He left him sitting on the ground, cursing in Italian, and ran after the black limousine, but by now it had backed into the road, was turning, driving away. Somewhere.

Sirens blaring. The cops coming.

Sullivan ran onto the sidewalk and around behind the house, and into the alley. He opened up the garbage can, grabbed his duffel. The little Sicilian police cars droned past the alley mouth, lights flashing. He pressed against the wall till they'd passed. Then he ran down the alley and lost himself in the maze of side streets, working his way downhill, toward the airport.

Legion returned from the phone, white-faced. He sat down at the kitchen table across from Ennio Montevori. They were in the kitchen of Ennio's brother's house, in the north of Palermo. Marcello stood against the wall, his arms folded, scowling.

"Well, what did you find out?" Ennio Montevori asked.

Legion swallowed hard. In a weak voice he said, "Do you have whiskey? Anything."

Marcello grunted and brought Legion a glass of liqueur. Legion downed it, then said, "My bodyguards have quit. They are afraid of the Specialist. They say Sullivan took Crackwell away to execute him. He killed Fabrizzio and thirteen others they threw against him. Thirteen!"

Marcello raised an eyebrow and grunted in approval.

Montevori looked thoughtful. Then he spoke to his brother in Italian. His brother gave a grunt that was meant for an affirmative, and went to call the airport. Then Montevori turned to Legion. He leaned earnestly across the table. "Now, listen to me and I will tell you something important. I have a feeling for these things: with so much killing around you, you cannot keep your business credibility. It is too messy. Too much attention attracted to you. You were a fool not to take care of your tenants. Here in Sicily, we take care of our people. Bad luck comes of such things. Our business association is at an end once this shipment is completed. I have some advice for you: take what money you have in New York, sell the shipment for money too, take it all, and run. But please, do not run to Sicily. Go to Tahiti, perhaps. Or Bangkok. Yes, I think so. Thailand. You have friends there."

"What are you telling me?" Legion asked in a strangled voice. "That you're deserting me?"

"We are looking for this killer. All Sicily will soon be looking for him. But you must leave the island. Go back to New York or directly to—"

Marcello returned to the kitchen and spoke to his brother in Italian.

Ennio Montevori nodded and turned to Legion again. "There are no flights to New York from Palermo this late. I think you should leave immediately. Two of my men are dead. Albano was a friend of my family. I want no more friends killed for your mistakes. You must go back to New York and salvage what is left of your business. Sell this shipment, take the money—after giving my partner in New York my share—and run to Thailand. You can go with the shipment, in the cargo planes, tonight. They will be leaving early, but I will make some calls, I will arrange for flight clearance. You can hire some men to take along to protect you. I will make some calls to find some for you. But no more of mine."

"But Ennio," Legion objected, "this is only temporary. We could weather this crisis, pal. Come out on top yet, huh? Come on, give me a chance to get back on my feet! I need this Sicilian connection!"

Montevori turned to his brother and asked, "Marcello, you heard me make a decision, did you not?"

"I heard."

"And once I make a decision, have you ever known me to change my mind?"

"Never," Marcello said grimly.

Montevori looked at Legion and spread his hands in a gesture of helplessness.

Sullivan's guess was that Legion would run, would run by plane, and would do it soon.

The airport was a small one, with a single large building, now mostly dark. There were only two cabdrivers out front. The land around the airport was brown and mostly flat. There was a grove of olive trees a hundred yards from the hurricane fence around the airports' landing strips. There was a small farmhouse on the other side of the olive trees, shuttered now, looking like a Hopi's adobe house to Sullivan.

Sullivan sat at the base of an olive tree in the grove, watching the airport and wishing he had some mosquito repellent and a heavier coat. His fingers were going numb on the cold iron of the Thompson in his lap. He fumbled one of his last Lucky Strikes out of his last pack and lit it, taking a chance on the flare being noticed by anyone who might be looking for him. The smoke would help keep the mosquitoes off, and help him think. He glanced up at the cold light of the stars. He could smell the sea in the breeze that rustled the leaves of the olive trees around him.

Fortunately, he'd had his wallet, credit cards, passport, and traveler's checks on him. All he'd left in the hotel room were some clothes, a razor, other odds and ends which would now have to be abandoned.

He looked at his watch. He'd long since changed it to Sicilian time. It glowed out: 12:01.

He'd stolen a motor scooter to get here. He'd ditched it a mile from here on a country road, and he'd walked cross-country to the airport. More than once he'd seen police cars humming through the streets, probably searching for him. He was used to eluding the police, and getting good at it. They hadn't seen him.

He suspected that Legion would have to run to New York, liquidate his holdings so far as was practical, and leave town quick. Sullivan would have to get him soon. But it wasn't going to be possible for Sullivan to simply use his round-trip ticket to get back to the States. He'd offended the local mob. They'd be looking for him at the airports.

Looking at the planes on the runway, waiting for clearance, he decided that there must be another way . . .

He made up his mind.

He got up, dusted himself off, carefully ground the cigarette out under his heel, and trotted out of the orchard, through a dusty field toward the airport.

18

Vengeance Served Cold

Bert, Danny, and Bill were sitting around the crew's cabin of an Easyair cargo jet, playing cards. The DC-9B was spiraling in over Canada, heading for JFK airport in New York. They were playing blackjack on a crate, one of the extra crates which couldn't fit into the main cargo hold.

Bert turned up his cards, and Bill, said, "Bert, you son of a bitch, that's the second blackjack you got in a row! Now, that ain't possible!"

"It's possible," Danny growled, "but it sure as hell ain't likely!" Both of them glared at Bert.

"You guys accusing me of cheating?" They just stared at him, so he changed the subject. "Hey, where's Larry?"

Danny frowned. He was a stocky thug with a Pancho Villa mustache and a black leather cap. He alternately cracked his knuckles and fingered the Smith and Wesson in his shoulder holster when he was nervous. "I dunno, he went back to the cargo hold before we took off. I figured he was loafing around back there. You know how he is about taking naps every chance he gets."

Bill and Bert, each one carrying an Uzi they'd bought in Sicily, were brothers. Bill was the older one, and bigger. He was pug-nosed, his eyes squinty, his mouth almost lipless. He had an oversize square head and brown hair. Bert looked like him except he was shorter, and he had a constellation of scars on his forehead from shotgun spray. His mother had pried the BB's out of the skin of his forehead with a pocketknife. He wore a blue leisure suit; Bill wore a yellow one.

Legion had hired these three and Larry in Sicily. They were Americans, free-lance killers working for an Italian shipping magnate. But they'd got homesick for Chicago. They figured to work for Legion awhile in New York, then split to the Windy City. Legion rode up front with the pilot.

Danny lit a cigarette and looked at the door to the cargo hold. The plane shuddered in turbulence, its engine roar muting slightly, then resurging.

"Hey, Larry!" Danny shouted at the closed metal door to the cargo hold.

The room they were in was shaped like a Quonset hut. It was about thirty feet long and twenty-five wide. There were several scallop-shaped windows looking out onto darkness. "Hey, Larry!" Bert shouted.

They waited. There was no answer from the cargo hold.

"When was the last time you saw him?" Bill asked.

Danny shrugged. "Right before we took off. Like I said—he went back there. It was late and he was yawning."

"I could do with some sleep myself," Bill said.

Bert said, "Mr. Legion don't want us to sleep. Like some gremlin's going to attack the plane up here or something." He snorted resentfully.

"Keep your voice down, Bert," Bill whispered, glancing toward the pilot cabin.

"He can't hear us, the door's closed . . . Hey—you think we left Larry behind?"

"Shit!" Danny began. "You think . . . ? Naw."

"Remember he was talking about going to get coffee? Maybe he did and we left him behind—all of us assuming he was in the back!"

Bill groaned. "Shit, Mr. Legion's going to be pissed! He gave us that advance, and Larry took his share!"

Bert said, "This is dumb, he's probably back there. I'll check it out." He got up and crossed to the door and banged on it. "Larry!"

A muffled voice shouted something in reply. Bert turned and grinned at the others. "He's in there. His voice sounds all weird—probably asleep. Or maybe he snuck some booze in!" He turned back to the door. "Hey, Larry, come on out!"

Another muffled reply no one could make out.

Bert said, "I knew it, the guy's got to be drunk."

He opened the door and went in, closing the door behind him.

Inside the cargo hold, Bert was staring at the opposite wall. Larry was sitting there, but he was staring at the ceiling, his mouth open. His arms hung limp at his sides. Bert took a step toward him and stopped, realizing that Larry was dead. He turned just in time to see the muzzle of a silenced Beretta spit flame, and then he didn't see anything ever again.

After twenty minutes or so, Bill found himself staring at the door to the cargo hold. "They been in there a long time."

"Yeah." Danny grinned. "And you know why? They're hogging the booze!"

Bill stood, frowning—and then reached out to grab a crate as the plane suddenly dropped in altitude. They were coming in over the airport, tilting into a turn. Bill waited till the plane leveled out for its final approach. Then he walked back to the cargo hold and opened the door.

He started to step through—then saw Larry and Bert staring at him from the opposite wall. Bert's eyes were closed, but he was looking at his brother with a new red eye in the middle of his forehead.

Bill threw himself back, and a bullet spanged into the bulkhead where he'd been standing. He scrabbled back into the cabin as Danny leapt to his feet, drawing the Smith and Wesson. Bill leapt for his Uzi on the crate.

And then the killer stepped through the door.

*   *   *

. . . Sullivan stepped through the door, the Thompson chattering in his hands, as Bill grabbed the Uzi and brought it up spraying.

The big submachine gun versus the little one. The big one filled the cabin with steel-jacketed lead rounds. The interior ricocheted the rounds back and forth, making a Mixmaster out of the cabin, so that Bill and Danny were Osterized with bullets, chopped to pieces, blood flying from them in every direction, spraying out in spirals as they spun about with the impact of the slugs, the red liquid splashing into the walls as if from one of those spinning lawn sprinklers spurting blood instead of water.

Two of the ports were blown out, but they were at a low altitude now, so the change in cabin pressure wasn't significant.

But the little submachine gun had drawn blood too. Sullivan leaned against the bulkhead, dizzy. He'd been hit in the left shoulder and the side. The slug in the shoulder had passed beneath the bone and above the lung, gone right through. It bled and it hurt—not much yet, the real pain would come later. The other round had slashed across his left side, just a deep graze. But he knew he could bleed to death from wounds like these.

He looked past the corpses to the front of the plane. Legion was up there. He must have heard the shooting and guessed that Sullivan had stowed away on his plane. He wouldn't dare come back here. And the pilot would be trying to set the plane down.

Sullivan knew Legion wouldn't let the pilot radio ahead for help. If the cops came, they'd be curious about all this, and they'd look more closely than usual at the cargo. They'd find the bags of heroin, two million dollars' worth, hidden in the padding of the furniture in the crates. Legion's connections in the customs department wouldn't help him get it through this time.

He crossed the cabin to a metal box on the wall. On the box was a red cross. He opened it and found disinfectant and pressure bandages. He stripped off his shirt and administered first aid. His left arm was going stiff. That was okay. He shot with his right.

Minutes later, as he put the shirt back on, complete with bullet hole, the plane touched down, its wheels making a sound like a turntable needle placed on a record for just a moment, then lifted off and placed down again, till the plane had landed completely. The plane grumbled down the runway, turned, and stopped.

Sullivan picked up the Thompson and checked the load. The drum was empty. No time to reload. He found the rifle, cocked it, and held it ready, facing the pilot's cabin. He heard a rattling sound, and a creaking, and then realized his mistake: there was another door out of the plane, beside the pilot. He cursed himself. Bullet wounds make you groggy, after the initial spurt of adrenaline.

He ran up front to the cabin, threw the door open, looked in at the cockpit. The dials glowed at him from the darkness. The cockpit was empty. There was a door to the left, tilted up, and a short flight of metal stairs going down. He looked through the door and saw the pilot climbing down, a big-nosed Italian with a long, sallow face and a nondescript uniform. Sullivan pointed the rifle at him and said, "Get back up here!"

The pilot scowled, but seeing the gun, did as he was told.

Sullivan could see Legion halfway across the blacktop already, running across the lighted runway toward one of the small squarish airport trucks. As Sullivan watched—and as the pilot climbed back into his seat, Sullivan behind him—Legion climbed up into the parked truck and started it. He drove toward the fences at the other end of the runway. It was designed for carrying cargo from planes—it was not a fast-moving vehicle. Legion was scared to try to go through customs, afraid that Sullivan would blow the whistle on him, tell them about the heroin in the plane.

Sullivan smiled, raising the gun, and told the pilot what he wanted him to do.

In the truck, driving frantically for the locked gate in the fence at the far end of the runway, Legion looked in the rearview mirror, expecting to see airport police coming after him. But it was dark, and the cops were distracted by something else: an Easyair cargo jet that was ignoring the orders of the air-traffic controllers and ground crews, its engines whinning as it rolled across two runways, over the grass strips between them, moving faster than a plane on the ground usually does, following the truck, following it on the ground, bearing down on it like a hawk hopping after a rabbit it missed on its dive.

Legion shouted incoherently, seeing one of his own cargo jets coming at him, looming over the truck, filling the mirror, covering the truck in its shadow.

He reached the fence and paused, looking out at the gate, wondering if he could ram through. And then there was a wrenching sound, a metallic grinding, and the roof buckled over him. The plane had overtaken him, its nose crushing the top of the truck. He wailed in fear and flung himself out the sidedoor, fell, skinning his knees, the pain slicing through the bone, then forced himself up, stumbling over the grass to the fence.

He was halfway up the fence when he felt the big steel-tendoned hand clamp down on his shoulder. He screamed, and the Specialist peeled him off his perch and threw him onto the ground.

"We'll go through the gate," the Specialist said. "I'll shoot the lock off, we'll go through, and we'll walk a ways cross-country, lose ourselves in the dark, and then maybe borrow somebody's car. How's that sound, Mr. Legion, hm?"

"Where are you taking me?" Legion demanded, trying to reestablish control. "This is stupid! Your're a soldier of fortune, right? So you work for who pays you, right?

Well, I'll pay you! I'll pay you a . . . a hundred thousand dollars! Twice what I was paying Fabrizzio!" He laughed nervously. "Sure! You see, I'm impressed with you! You . . . you're really all they say you are! I . . . I was wrong about you! So, uh, I want you on my team! Okay, two hundred thou, and I'll make you half-partner in everything! We'll even fix up that building for your friends and I'll . . . I'll halve their rents, they can stay as long as they want, and, uh . . ."

He broke off, not liking the sound of the Speicalist's soft laughter.

"The city'll fix up that building," Sullivan said. "It'll seize your assets once you're dead, or even if you're not. See, I radioed in from that plane about what was in the cargo hold, hidden in the furniture. The customs inspectors will be all over that plane. And all your associates are through, too. Both Krinsky and Crackwell sang, like pretty little birds."

"Okay, okay . . . but I can still pay you. I've got money stashed away in my house."

"Good, I'll go pick it up later. Donate it to a heroin user's rehabilitation house I know of. Where is it?"

"In the wall behind the desk. Okay? You pull out the wall socket, and you'll find it. All right? So you can let me go, huh?"

"I'm not going to kill you," Sullivan said. "You're going to kill yourself."

"What . . . what do you mean?"

Sullivan was driving through Harlem. Legion was tied up in the back, his arms pulled behind him and lashed to the door of the Chevrolet station wagon Sullivan had "borrowed" from the driveway of a suburban house. Rain drizzled down in a fine, bone-chilling mist. A sharper wind rose, whining down the streets, and the temperature dropped, turning the coating of water on everything into a film of black ice.

The temperature dropped and dropped, and continued to fall all through the night. It was going to be a cold, cold night.

Sullivan pulled up in front of a tenement in the darkest part of Harlem.

He looked at a slip of paper he carried in his wallet. On the paper was a list of addresses Bonnie had given him. "Yeah," Sullivan said, "this is one of the buildings you own. It's on a list of buildings that you own. The tenants here have complained that you haven't been repairing the furnace. They can't afford to do it themselves, and anyway, you're obligated by law to do it, Legion. But you didn't. And the people in this building are mighty cold this winter. I expect most of them are getting by with extra blankets or by using the heat from the kitchen gas stove. But some of them won't make it through the winter. Unless, of course, the city takes over the building. And it will. In the meantime, let's you and me inspect that furnace."

"Sure, sure," Legion said desperately, "anything you say. I'll fix it, I can see I've been messing up, I'll fix it—"

Sullivan laughed at Legion's pathetic duplicity, and dragged him out of the car, across the slippery street. The block looked almost deserted. It was trash-cluttered, graffiti-choked, ugly as a war zone.

Sullivan dragged Legion into the building. It was easy: the front door was missing.

Sullivan shoved Legion down the stairs. He went bumping and groaning down, but landed in the cellar without breaking any bones.

Sullivan turned on the basement light. "Surprised to see that's working," he said. A rat wriggled sinuously into a hole in the wall.

Sullivan dragged Legion to the stone-cold furnace and lashed him to it with wires he found heaped in a corner. Lashed him very, very thoroughly. It took him a while, because his fingers were numb from the cold.

Legion whined, "Look, you can't leave me here. I'll freeze to death!"

"Will you? That's the landlord's fault. If this furnace were working, you'd live through the night. As it is, I have a feeling you're not going to make it."

Legion tried to scream for help, but Sullivan gagged him. He tied Legion's limbs down so he couldn't bang around and make noise.

Sullivan yawned and stretched. He was tired. "See you, Legion," he said, going up the steps. But then, pausing at the top of the stairs, he said musingly, "I guess I *won't* be seeing you, though? Will I?"

And he switched off the light to the soft sound of Legion's muffled cries.

Four days later, Bonnie was released from the hospital. When she was well enough to travel, Sullivan took her to Hawaii, where they lay on the white sands, both of them convalescing from their wounds. And drinking in the warmth of the Hawaiian sun.

The same day they arrived in Hawaii, a furnace repairman, sent by the city of New York, walked down to the cellar door in a certain building in Harlem. He opened the door, switched on the light, and went down the stairs.

He found a dead man tied to the cold furnace, his frozen skin blue, his frozen eyes staring in horror.

DON'T MISS . . .

The following is an exciting excerpt
from the next novel in the
Specialist series from Signet:

THE SPECIALIST #9
Vengeance Mountain

Jack Sullivan maneuvered the rented Cutlass into the
exit lane, his eyes never leaving the two targets in their
late-model midnight-blue Lincoln Continental. He'd followed them all the way from Manhattan, always careful
to keep a few cars behind them. As he turned off the
highway, a small humorless grin creased his face. It
shouldn't be long now, he thought.

This job turned out to be surprisingly clean, Sullivan
thought. Unlike most of his other missions. He'd had
the time to plan, to stalk his targets and let them lead
him to their den so he could complete the job in one
attack. "Efficiency killing," Sullivan murmured to himself.

But as he drove down the tree-lined country road
thirty yards behind the Lincoln, the smile faded from
Sullivan's face. Rule Number One of the Specialist: Get
cocky and get killed. Don't take anything for granted.
There could be more to contend with than just these
two slime-buckets. No job is ever that neat.

The Lincoln came to a fork in the road and bore to the
left without hesitating. Sullivan slowed to make it look
like he was reading the sign, then took the road to the
left, the road to Ashokan.

He'd been very careful not to blow his cover, but now that they were the only two cars on the road, Sullivan had to be as inconspicuous as possible. That's why he had rented the white sedan and dressed in running shoes, jeans, a tan turtleneck, and a well-worn brown corduroy jacket. Just another suburban nature-lover out to see the fall foliage.

He glanced over to the navy-blue Cordura backpack on the seat next to him. Lunch.

Lake Williams stretched out to Sullivan's left, reflecting the golds and russets of the trees along its banks. The scum had picked some beautiful country for their dirty little operation. But Sullivan had long gotten used to the fact that parasites usually had pretty good taste when it came to picking a nest. No one ever suspects that something as ugly as a child pornography operation could exist in such a beautiful place. It can't happen here. Yeah, right.

The blue Lincoln sped along the lake for about seven miles, then turned right onto a narrow road that cut into the woods. Sullivan pulled over and stopped by the lake for a minute before he turned down the road. He looked up at the chipped whitewashed road sign. Old Indian Road.

Sullivan knew he couldn't lose them on this deserted road, not if they were in a Lincoln. There were no houses, no side roads, just woods. After about a half a mile, Sullivan spotted a weather-beaten tin post box by the side of the road. Slowing down, he saw a narrow dirt drive overgrown with ferns. An old ramshackle house stood at the end of the drive. Its windows had been boarded up and part of the roof had caved in. It was a sharp contrast to the shiny new luxury sedan pulling around the back.

Bingo.

Sullivan pressed the accelerator and continued down the road another quarter-mile or so until he found a suitable copse of trees in which to hide his car. Switching off the ignition, he reached for the knapsack. He rummaged around in it a bit, then found what he was looking for. The .44 Automag emerged slowly from his knapsack like a cobra from a snake-charmer's basket.

Sullivan weighed the Automag in his hand. It was a very special weapon, without question the most powerful automatic pistol on the market. Its extra long 165mm barrel length gave it a sleek, snakelike profile, though it also made it cumbersome when carried under a jacket in a holster. Of course, this wasn't a problem for someone as large as Sullivan. He found a full clip in his backpack and slammed it into the weapon. It held eight cartridges, cartridges designed uniquely for the Automag—.44 revolver bullets fitted in cut-down 7.62mm NATO rifle cartridge cases. The manufacture listed it as a hunting weapon, and that's just what Sullivan was using it for. Hunting.

He got out of the car, tucked the Automag into his belt, slung the backpack over his shoulder, and disappeared into the woods, heading for his quarry.

Preminger peered through field glasses from his perch in a tree behind the dilapidated house. He'd staked out the house days ago, and this was the second boring afternoon he'd spent waiting for the attack. It was a relief to see Babcock's blue Lincoln pull into the drive. For one thing, it relieved the incredible monotony of watching the squirrels watching him; for another, Preminger would finally get to see the kiddie porn king in the flesh, Harry Babcock.

But when Babcock rolled out from behind the wheel of the Lincoln, Preminger was disappointed. He'd expected a flashy dude with dark wavy hair, a pearly smile, and an Italian-cut silk suit. Sort of a sleazy Victor Mature type. What emerged from the car was an overweight, bald guy in his early fifties wearing a thick gray cardigan sweater and round gold-rimmed glasses. His brows had a sympathetic slant and he looked totally harmless—sort of a cross between Mr. Rogers and an accountant.

Babcock's bodyguard was more in character, though. Greasy black hair, dangling cigarette, butternut leather trenchcoat, pointy gray suede shoes. From the unprofessional way he held open the front of his coat, he may as well have worn a sign that read I'M CARRYING A CANNON.

After Babcock and his bodyguard went into the house through the cellar hatch, Preminger scanned the nearby woods. He spotted movement. He focused his glasses and saw a pair of huge shoulders and a dark head of hair with white-streaked sideburns moving carefully toward the house. Preminger watched the man stalk up to the side of the house and peer through the windows on the ground floor.

"Well, if it isn't the Specialist," Preminger murmured to himself. "Okay, Sullivan, let's see what you can do."

Babcock hit the lights in the basement of the shabby house, illuminating his newest studio. Instead of the gloomy, cobweb-ridden cellar the old house should have had, it had wall-to-wall carpeting and expensive high-tech furnishings. One end of the room hosted a lounge complete with a fully stocked bar, plush sofas, and a six-foot video projection screen. At the other end was the work area where the movies were made. A big black movie camera sat on a tripod like a giant spider staring dead-eyed at the set—a double bed on a platform spread with red satin sheets. The backdrop was a screen painted to resemble a kid's bedroom with a toy shelf on the wall and frilly curtains on the painted windows.

"Hey, this is some set-up you got here, Mr. Babcock," the bodyguard marveled as he came down the cellar steps.

"Close the cellar door behind you, Lenny. And lock it." Babcock didn't want anyone getting in or out when he worked.

Babcock sorted through his key ring as he went into the other part of the cellar, the part where the coal bin used to be. The walls in this room were lined with floor-to-ceiling shelving full of video tapes and film cannisters. His inventory of kiddie porn films. His specialty.

He walked up to a steel door that sealed off what used to be the coal bin and unlocked the dead-bolt. A dim light from within spilled out into the basement as Babcock peered in to check on his latest star. A little girl, no more than ten years old, gazed at Babcock through the tangled strands of her golden blond hair. She sat trembling on a narrow bed, her legs tucked underneath her. She was completely naked.

"I told you I'd come back, didn't I?" Babcock said with a reassuring smile.

The little girl didn't respond, but Babcock was used to this kind of behavior from his leading ladies. He stepped over the dolls and board games strewn over the floor and opened the half-sized refrigerator. "Ran out of food, I see. I didn't think a little sweetie like you could eat that much. Well, it's better that you're a little hungry. You work better when you're hungry, did you know that? First we'll do a little work and then we can have some cookies and milk. How does that sound?"

Babcock had a knack for making whatever he said sound warm and reassuring to a child. Some would say he had a natural way with kids. That's how he got his stars to do what no other pornographer had ever gotten children to do on film. You name it, Babcock had filmed it. Even kiddie snuff porn.

And if his little actors and actresses didn't like the script . . . well, Babcock just disciplined them. Very severely.

"Come on, sweetie. It's showtime." Babcock took the little girl by the hand and led her out to the set. Scared out of her wits, she followed like a zombie.

"Aw-right!" Lenny yelled from the sofa where he'd settled in with a double scotch. "A little tits and ass, and I do mean little."

"Shut up, Lenny!" Babcock snapped. "I don't put up with distractions when I work. Isn't that right, Melinda?"

His tone had changed instantly from venomous to sugary when he addressed the little girl.

"Sorry, Mr. Babcock. I'll be quiet."

"See to it that you do."

Babcock led the little girl to the big bed and told her to get up. He then went to his "prop department," a corner of the basement cluttered with boxes and racks of negligees, corsets, and sequined gowns all in various child sizes. He dug through one of the boxes and came up with what he was looking for. A twelve-inch, baby-pink dildo.

"Okay, Melinda," he said, holding out the dildo to the little girl like a lollypop, "now if you really want those cookies we were talking about, all you have to do is—"

Everything suddenly went black. The lights had gone out. Melinda screamed in terror, and Lenny started to curse.

"Damn," Babcock spat. "Lenny, listen to me. There's a flashlight behind the bar. Get it so we can find the fuse box."

The bodyguard was still cursing under his breath as he reached into his pocket for his butane lighter. He flicked his Bic and nearly pissed his pants when he saw the killer eyes set deep in the grim, scarred face eerily lit from below, an executioner's face looming right in front of him.

"Shit!" Lenny yelped as he fumbled for his piece, but the Specialist beat him to the draw. The strobe-flash from the Automag lit the room for a split second as Sullivan blew the greaseball away at point-blank range, the 7.62mm slug ripping through his breastbone to make hash of his heart before smashing out his back. Lenny's guts and blood splashed messily on the wall behind him.

In the darkness, Sullivan heard Babcock's stumbling footsteps on the wooden stairway that led to the first floor. Remembering the layout of the room, Sullivan leapt over a sofa and dashed up the steps after the pornographer. He caught up with the huffing fat man in the dusty upstairs hallway and brought him down by smashing Babcock's head with the butt of his gun.

Sullivan unslung his backpack as he looked down at the heap of blubber on the dirty floor. He unzipped a side pocket and pulled out a pair of handcuffs, then gathered up Babcock's wrists and bound them behind his back.

"Don't go away," Sullivan said as he shoved the Automag in his belt and went back downstairs.

Switching on the lights, he saw the little girl clutching the obscene satin sheets, shivering in fear. Sullivan started to say something, but then decided against it. Babcock had conned this poor kid with his Mr. Gentle routine, so she sure wouldn't trust him if he came on to her the same way.

"Hi," he said casually, walking slowly toward her. "Are you cold? You look cold."

The girl didn't answer. The long scar across Sullivan's right cheek from his eye to the jawline frightened her. He was an imposing figure, standing more than six feet tall, and his massive build filled the small set.

Sullivan opened his backpack and pulled out a small orange jumpsuit and a pair of leather-soled slipper socks. "Here," he said, tossing them onto the bed. "You can have these." He didn't want to approach her until he was sure he had her confidence.

He reached into his pack and came up with something wrapped in tin foil. Melinda stared at him in curiosity. He unwrapped it, then made a face. "Peanut butter and jelly again? I hate peanut butter and jelly. Do you want it?"

Sullivan held out the sandwich and stepped forward. She reached out for the food in desperation. From the way she devoured it, it was clear she hadn't eaten in days.

Melinda let him help her on with the clothes as she finished the sandwich. Next he produced a box of Animal Crackers. He opened the box, popped one in his mouth, then handed the rest to Melinda.

"I don't like this place," he said, looking around. "In fact, I *hate* this place. I'm going. You want to come?"

Melinda nodded, her mouth full, her blue eyes as big as saucers.

Sullivan picked her up, and immediately she threw her arms around his neck. "It's okay, Melinda," he said softly. "The nightmare is over."

He brought her upstairs, covering her eyes so she wouldn't have to see Babcock who was just coming around. Gently Sullivan lowered her out the same window he'd used to come in. "Now, Melinda, you wait over there by that big tree, okay? I'll be out in a minute."

Melinda nodded and did as he asked.

"Hey . . . hey you! What the fuck do you think you're doing?" Babcock shouted. "Where's my kid?"

"*Your* kid?" Sullivan said, grabbing Babcock by the collar and dragging him back downstairs like a sack of potatoes.

Babcock yelped when he saw the six-inch hole in his bodyguard's chest. Blood and shreds of organs were splattered all over his nice pastel-colored lounge.

"I suppose in a way they were all your kids, Babcock. That's the scam, right? You adopt homeless kids, then put 'em to work in your porno flicks. If they don't cooperate, they don't eat. And if they still don't play ball, then they get beat."

"No, no, you got me wrong, man," Babcock blithered. "I just do soft-core stuff. Honest. I don't hurt them."

"Sure, tell me another one."

Babcock squirmed helplessly as Sullivan dragged him to the back room where the films and cassettes were stored. Sullivan stood him up and shoved him against the shelves. Babcock's nose smashed against the edge of one shelf, then he fell into a heap, video tapes raining down around him.

"Hey, come on, man," Babcock pleaded. "Take it easy."

Sullivan ignored him while he read some of the titles

printed on the spines of the video cassette boxes. "Let's see what you've got here—*Babes in Toyland . . . Dick and Jane Have a Ball . . . Bang-Bang, You're Dead . . . Lassie, Come Home . . .*" Sullivan bounced the films off Babcock's belly as he read the titles.

"Look, man, you're destroying my inventory. Name your price. Just tell me what the fuck you want."

"I'm already being paid, Babcock. Paid to hang up your ass."

"What . . . ?"

"Don't look so surprised, Babcock. Do you remember a little girl named Ginger Hayes? You must remember her. She's the reason you had to leave California and set up shop here in New York."

"I don't know what the hell you're talking about." The sweat streaming down Babcock's fat face indicated otherwise."

"Let me refresh your memory. One day you picked up the paper and read about this couple in Sausalito who died in a suicide pact. They had a little girl, seven years old. The paper said there were no surviving relatives and the kid had to go to a foster home. Perfect kid for you, you figured, so you adopted her, became her legal guardian. You'd done that number before plenty of times. The adoption agencies in California actually thought you were a real prince taking all these kids in. Man, did you ever have them buffaloed."

"You've got the wrong guy. That's not me," Babcock whimpered.

"It's you, all right. That 'script girl' you sent out to dispose of the body testified to it. She got cold feet and ran to the police. I've seen the pictures of Ginger's body. What did you use on her? A rubber truncheon?"

"Noooo," Babcock whined. "Let me explain—"

"No, let me explain it to you, Babs. Or should I say Henry Bucknell? That's the name you were using when you offed Ginger Hayes. See, what you didn't know was that Ginger's father had a brother in Alaska. Yeah, and when Uncle Dave got wind of what you did to his niece, he got pretty crazy. Uncle Dave's one of those rugged mountain types, so he wasn't about to let the law deal with you. He knows that guys like you have a way of slipping away from justice. That's why he hired me to do the job."

Sullivan dug into his backpack and came up with some nylon clothesline, which he used to tie Babcock to one of uprights of the shelves bolted to the wall. Babcock blubbered like an infant as Sullivan opened one film cannister after another and dumped them on the porno king. When Babcock was up to his chest in spilled film and cassettes, Sullivan went back to his bag and pulled out a two-quart Thermos bottle.

"Uncle Dave told me his one wish is that you burn in hell. And since you store your masters and your inventory right here, we can make Uncle Dave's dream come true and get rid of your whole dirty operation in one neat package."

Sullivan unscrewed the top of the Thermos bottle, releasing blue gasoline fumes. He calmly splashed gas on top of the mountan of porn, then tossed the Thermos aside. Reaching into his inside pocket, Sullivan took out a pack of Lucky Strikes and stuck one between his lips.

"Uncle Dave will be very happy," Sullivan muttered, making the unlit cigarette jump.

Ignoring the screaming man on the floor, Sullivan lit his cigarette and tossed the burning match behind him as he left. He heard the *phoomp* of the gas igniting and the piercing screams of the condemned man. Sullivan's only worry was that Melinda might hear the screams outside. She'd already gone through enough.

Little Melinda took Sullivan's hand and followed him through the woods back to his car. She didn't seem to be afraid of him, but Sullivan hoped her trust wasn't based solely on a food bribe. A lot of people believed that trust only got you into trouble, but Sullivan couldn't disagree more. If you couldn't put your trust in someone, something in life, you might as well be dead. He just hoped to God that Melinda's experience with that slime Babcock hadn't done any permanent damage and hardened her soul for good.

But as they strolled through the orange-gold leaves covering the ground, something interrupted Jack Sullivan's train of thought. He sensed it instinctively before he actually heard anything. It was a sixth sense he'd picked up in 'Nam when he'd led lurps deep into Viet Cong territory. Lurps—long-range reconnaissance patrols—were basically suicide missions, jungle hikes to "Camp Dead Dog," because once you got out of radio range of your base camp, you could forget about calling for helicopter support if you got into a jam. All you had on lurps was what you and your men carried on their backs. If you stood any chance of surviving a long-range mission, you had to find the enemy before they found you. One of the Specialist's specialties was this gift he had for sensing enemy presence even in the thickest jungle. That's how he he'd been able to run countless lurp missions and always come back to tell about it.

He sensed somebody tracking him right now.

They kept walking, Sullivan smiling at Melinda, pretending that his guard was down and that he didn't suspect a thing. But his mind was working like a computer, sizing up the terrain, measuring distances, weighing the options and the risks. As Sullivan saw it, there were two imperatives: getting the girl out of harm's way and not tipping his hand too soon.

When they got to the car, Sullivan opened the passenger door and let Melinda in. He unslung the blue backpack from his shoulder, reached in, and pulled out another Thermos bottle.

"What's that?" Melinda asked.

Sullivan looked at her, then looked at the Thermos clutched in his fist. "Chocolate milk," he said. "You like chocolate milk, don't you?"

Melinda nodded eagerly.

"Okay, this is for you then. Save a little for me, though."

"Okay," she smiled.

"Say, Melinda, will you do me a favor? See that lever right there." He pointed to the hood release under the dashboard. "Pull that lever for me, okay?"

"Okay."

Sullivan went around to the front of the car and lifted the hood.

Preminger couldn't see the Specialist from where he was crouched behind a stand of tall ferns. His view was blocked by the raised hood of the Cutlass. What the hell is he doing? Preminger wondered. Then it occurred to him that the car may have been equipped with a hidden kill switch that cut off the ignition and prevented the engine from starting. Lots of people had them in their cars to guard against car theft; Preminger didn't give it a second thought.

He relaxed his grip on the .44 Bulldog in his hand. He had no intention of tangling with the Specialist, but from what he'd heard, the guy could be a maniac. He had heard the blood-curdling screams from the old house, and there was no doubt in his mind that Sullivan was lethal, so a little caution was in order. But what the hell was he doing under the hood so—

And then Preminger had only darkness to contemplate.

When Preminger came to, he was flat on his back trying to focus his eyes. Two looming shapes standing over him finally came together. It was the imposing form of Jack Sullivan emptying the cartridges out of Preminger's revolver.

While Preminger thought Sullivan was fiddling under the hood of the car, the Specialist had slipped back into the woods, circled around behind "the enemy," cold-cocked him, and disarmed him. Tossing the empty gun aside, Sullivan bent his knees and tensed his hands. The grim look in Sullivan's eyes warned Preminger that if he tried something stupid, he could break him in half with his bare hands.

"Who are you and why are you following me?" Sullivan growled. "And remember—you lie, you die."

Preminger rubbed the back of his head but wisely didn't try to sit up. "My name's Preminger. I'm a private detective."

"Yeah? What else?"

"I was hired by a group of people who want to engage your services. They heard your fee is pretty steep, so they wanted to have you checked out before they put up that kind of cash. Some of them were skeptical about your reputation. They hired me to find out first-hand how effective you really are." Preminger rotated his head and winced with pain. "I'd say you're pretty fucking effective," he grunted.

Sullivan didn't say a word; his gaze never wandered from his captive. His inner computer was racing, analyzing this Preminger. Private dicks come in all colors, he reasoned. Just like everything else, there are good ones, bad ones, and useless ones. Preminger had to have balls to take this assignment, but there was something unmistakeably shady about him. Still, Sullivan's gut feelings told him that Preminger was telling the truth now, and Sullivan had learned long ago to trust his gut feelings because they were seldom wrong.

"What exactly do your clients want me to do for them?"

"Get vengeance for them. There are twenty-nine people in this group, and they all lost someone close to them. All murdered by the same killer."

Sullivan didn't have to hear any more. In his mind, he was already on the job.

Thrilling Reading from SIGNET